Down Island

A novel exploring time and light in the eighteenth latitude

By Bob Tis

Cover art by
Stephen Smalzel, Salida Colorado

Published by Mooshka Press
P.O. Box 84
Cruz Bay, St. John, U.S. Virgin Islands
00831

ISBN 0-9713933-1-1

9 780971 393318

Printed in the United States Virgin Islands by St. Thomas Graphics

For Nichole

Enjoy!!

Bob

2-18-2010

Down Island

To Doris

Down Island

Preface

This novel is an invention of the imagination and pure fiction. There are no intended portraits of actual people or places in this book. The characters exist only on these pages and in the reader's mind to help create the atmosphere necessary to tell a fictional story set in the Caribbean. Any similarities that any of the creations in this book may arouse in the reader's mind are purely coincidental and do not deserve any further study.

Fictional freedoms have been taken with the names of well known people, places and events in hopes of creating an authoritative autobiographical tone.

I would like to express my sincere thanks to the people who unknowingly gave me the time, space, energy and inspiration to write this small book.

Down Island

"The nature of a work of Art
is not a part, nor yet
a copy of the real world
(as we commonly understand
that phrase).
But a world in itself,
independent, complete, autonomous;
and to possess it fully
you must enter that world
conform to its laws
and ignore for the time the beliefs,
aims and particular conditions
which belong to you
in the other world of reality."

Oxford Lectures on Poetry
Professor H. Bradley 1901

Down Island

PART I
chapter I

Reservations

Now it's come to this.

I'm sitting on worn out blue cushions in the cabin of a dilapidated 30 year old, O'Day sailboat. I am alone and floating quietly in the middle of a mooring field in the Caribbean. The harbor is full of similar weary sailing vessels. Forgotten dreams.

I am afloat in Fort Bay Harbor on the far East End of St. Simon, a remote U.S. territory in the Caribbean's Lesser Antilles. It is the end of the line.

I am staring intently at a hand-held VHF radio on the opposite settee.

I am sweating in the cool of the evening.

The sun has just set and a rapidly waxing moon has broken the horizon. Enormous, egg shaped and rising over the tranquil British Virgin Islands, the natural satellite of the earth is still catching the sinking rays of the sun. I can hear the barflies onshore buzzing at Fatty Kegs bar. They started collecting themselves at Happy Hour and now they are beginning to unravel in public, all over Fort Bay.

I am silent and measure the passing minutes with distaste.

An hour passes and my painful stare remains locked on the radio.

I look briefly up from the hand-held and out through the companionway door to see a full complement of stars beginning to decorate the infinite night sky.

I'm 37. I used to be a professional, or I tell people that. Now I'm waiting for a faceless but familiar voice to hail me on the marine band radio. They will ask me if we have dinner reservations.

This is where I make my call.

If things seem cool, I will say something like, "Yes, Biff, we have reservations for six," or some other similar code word.

Then I will wait exactly three hours, during which time I will sweat some more, watch the radio which is ever-tuned to channel 71, and wonder why this is my story.

Eventually I will row over to an old black Starcraft "go-fast" ski-boat with nearly new twin Merc 90's on the back. It looks shabby but it is a well-oiled machine. I will zoom out of Fort Bay Harbor on a rhumb line for Norman Island, the scenic and still uninhabited "Cay" where an aged and fragile Robert Louis Stevenson was fabled to have set his epic Treasure Island.

Halfway between here and that isolated nowhere I will slow to a near stop and like a midnight lobsterman I will haul maybe a half dozen bales on board. Then I will jet off to an isolated cove on Norman Island's southern tip. It might take a few trips to haul the dope up to a small cave, but once I am done, I'm finished.

A late model sloop that looks like it belongs to the Moorings Company will come by the next day and the drugs will go on board in life preserver bags and be destined for points between Key West and Kennebunk by mid-afternoon.

I'm paid quite well for my part in this arrangement. The risks seem minimal to me, partly because I've been here for like forever and I know firsthand that there is nobody out there watching.

The Coast Guard only has one boat right now. It comes to Roach Harbor on the West side of St. Simon sometimes, but mostly just to do PFD checks and to inspect the growing number of car barges.

We keep that boat well monitored. The local water police don't go out at night. They can't swim and they are scared of smugglers.

The cache drop in this particular arrangement is technically in the British Virgin Islands anyway, just out of the Fed's range. Norman Island is British and they don't have many water police in the BVI just yet. If they did things would change fast.

Bottom line, right now anyway, nobody is going to mess with an unlit speedboat at night. There are too many guns and crazy people on the water to pay any West Indian lawman to do nighttime boat stops.

I pack heat but I don't brag about it, in fact, nobody knows anything about this.

I don't have any papers on the speedboat or the O'Day. I know people wonder who owns the speedboat. I let some old West Indian men use it to go fishing so the conjecture is ripe. I pay my mechanic to keep his mouth shut. There is always somebody watching in Fort Bay, but not the police.

I usually let somebody live on the O'Day too, just to keep the boat and appearances, up. The escutcheon is blank and there are no registration numbers. Nobody asks questions in Fort Bay.

The problem is that most of the white people in Fort Bay who would want to live on a crappy old fiberglass boat are career drunks. I was so worried the last guy would drink himself to near death on board and drown after a midnight piss that I just recently had to move him along. I had visions of him washing up on the shore by the fancy restaurant with his zipper still open and his hand in place. My former tenant might get rolled by some locals in Fort Bay, but at least he won't drown, I reasoned to him.

"Okay Don," he told me last week. "But will you help me move?"

Drunks in the Islands take orders well. Just don't try and get between them and their morning Budweiser. It continually amazes me how orderly and even trustworthy they can be. Tonight in the candlelight of the salon I consider the way Steinbeck bet on the drunk in *The Winter of Our Discontent* and won as a cacophony of bar sounds from Fatty Kegs routinely bounce and echo around the harbor. Their yelps are as reliable as the crickets and cicadas.

Time is ample and stationary on my floating perch and the darkness pervasive as clouds cover the moon.

The last tenant on board this floating Clorox bottle, which I dubbed The Fantasy some years back, kept this old boat clean and fairly neat. He left all sorts of books on board which I assume he was too sloshed to read. I started flipping through them a minute ago but I am way too freaked out for study.

I've recently become involved with this 25 year-old girl who makes jewelry. Her name is Jenny and she rents a small shop in Roach Harbor. She worries me because she isn't a drunk.

We started running into each other at Superman's Beach, out in Jumbala Bay, early in the morning. We had been walking the same trail out from Roach Harbor to take a swim just after dawn. We clicked and things started happening fast.

Naturally she asked what I did for a living.

Most people know I work at *The Melee,* the local weekly newspaper. St. Simon is small and everyone knows everyone at least by face but more often by reputation.

My name is well known. I'm Don Hunger, the newspaper guy. You know, that reporter who smiles absurdly when he's drunk and spends his days throwing a Frisbee around at Jumbala Bay beach.

Nobody asks much more. But Jenny seemed smart from the beginning and I sort of trusted her because of it.

Now, in my dark isolation aboard The Fantasy, I'm wondering just how smart this little brown-eyed girl from New England could be. I admit to myself that I feel queasy but the sweating doesn't stop.

My particular drug run is not new. My uncle gave it to me much the way neighborhood kids hand down a paper route. He retired a very rich man in 1982. His friend Carlos is still involved in the larger operation somehow, but I can't really remember the last time I saw him. I bet it's been a dozen years. But I know he is watching. I know I am a small cog in a lucrative, dangerous and evil machine.

But the deal is too good to pass up. I answer my call on the radio, take a midnight run and an envelope jammed full of fifty dollar bills appears at my house in Roach Harbor around Christmas time. It is a very smooth operation.

No one seems to retire from this business. I have been hearing the same West Indian voice ask if we have dinner reservations, or some such thing, for a dozen years. Sometimes we only do one or two runs a year. The most pick-ups I have done in one year was a few years back when I made a half dozen runs. That netted me about fifty grand.

The "restaurant" has never been closed either, or at least not since a very scary drug bust in the Seventies. People still talk about that bust but anyone who had any real relation to it has completely scattered. It was that scary.

Carlos and my Uncle Eugene quickly filled a void after that bust and basically disappeared into thin air. Sometimes old timers ask me about them and I just shrug.

My instructions are simple. Pick up the bales, drop off the bales and don't talk to anyone. Close the "restaurant" if anyone, anyone at all, even has the faintest idea there is a drop-off planned.

This morning on the trail to the beach the smart girl, her friends call her Jen but I prefer Jenny, asked what I was doing later.

I didn't hesitate and I didn't lie.

I said I had to check on a boat out in Fort Bay. She of course thought it strange that I never mentioned to her that I had or took care of a boat.

What kind of boat?" she asked.

"Sail boat," I stuttered.

She nodded like I was from the moon.

"Okay," she said, exaggerating hurt, "I'll see ya, when I see ya."

On the far East End, Fort Bay is nearly an hour away from her jewelry store in Roach Harbor, the center of commerce and tourism on St. Simon.

Checking on a boat can take a couple hours or a couple days as spring turns into summer. Hurricanes begin welling up off the coast of Africa in June and if you are not prepared you will lose your boat. I know as I sit here sweating that I left it vague and she didn't press me. Maybe if she did press me, I wouldn't be this freaked.

My mind first started racing after lunch. I replayed as many of our numerous conversations as my brain would allow. I puzzled over her lack of questions. It was almost as if she was trying not to make me nervous, or she was acting. I mean what is a Vassar graduate doing living year round in St. Simon? She certainly can't be that interested in a rapidly balding reporter for a weekly newspaper. Her jewelry isn't that good that she could be making enough money to really want to stay in the Caribbean full time. Don't they train those girls from the fancy schools to follow the money?

I loathe paranoia. I stopped smoking pot a decade ago to keep my head in check.

Confidence is funny and this is a confidence game I play a few times a year.

The yahoos you see in these Islands are just that, yahoos and mamas boys. Most of them have trust funds or are just serious substance abusers. I know the people who are in the business from my uncle, from my father and through Carlos. They come and go as quietly as possible and blend in as best they can.

The people in the business don't want to be here. It's too weird. You can feel it in the air sometimes. The people in the business would much rather be at the ski-house in Telluride or up in Maine, where they have a different life. The islands are simply where they make their money.

I don't know why Jenny is here. She showed up on a sailboat and liked it, that's her story. Two years later she has dusted off some of the more popular yahoos on the St. Simon stage and last week she started sleeping with me.

Now I think she might be a cop.

Unfortunately I find a few nips of Jagermeister behind the books left over from my last floating tenant. Now I have to stare at the handheld radio and the little green bottles. I know in my heart I am as weak, if not weaker, than the loaded denizens I hear at Fatty Kegs. This tugs at me as I stare at the liquor.

I know you don't drink before work or cards but I would like to calm my nerves. Every run is a gamble.

"I've been doing this too long to appear rattled on the radio," I tell myself, eyes on the little green bottle. Just then I hear a familiar voice call for sailing vessel Fantasy

I pick up the radio and make the decision as I bring it to my lips.

"Reservations are canceled," I say without hesitation. "Foxy's all full up, over."

Somewhere in Gorda Sound a small crew preparing to dump a few bales of Columbia's finest cocaine into the ocean probably can't believe their ears. I'm having trouble believing it myself.

The delivery crew must have backup plans, I am sure they do, but I also know they haven't had to use back up plans on this run for decades. They will probably have to sail through the night for St. Barts with their illegal cargo. They very well might have to dump a half million dollars worth of drugs into the deep blue. That is their problem now. This "restaurant" is closed due to female curiosity and male paranoia.

My share in this is dead, but like I said, this is my call. I am spooked by this girl and I clearly need a new life.

"Come back, Fantasy," I hear on the scratchy handheld. "Did you say our reservations are canceled?, over."

"The restaurant is closed for a private party," I reply reaching for a nip, "Over and out."

Down Island

chapter 2
Paper Route

On Monday we do the paper route.

I look forward to these whirlwind tours of our small island all week. Because the hills are so precipitous and the potholes so prevalent, the Publisher often rents a late model Japanese jeep he can't afford for the delivery, if only to allow his dilapidated Chevy Blazer hope for another year on the road.

The Melee is the weekly newspaper for the Caribbean island of St. Simon and has been, in one form or another, since 1968. The Publisher and I get it done through the course of a very casual workweek that roughly spans Wednesday to Saturday.

On Sundays we paste up the paper, make up misleading headlines for the stories and layout the local copy and ads. A real newspaper might call Sunday a production day but that is a little ambitious for our operation. Writing the paper is actually pretty fun by Sunday. The goal is to give the camera ready proof of the paper to our Operations Manager, a native St. Simonian known simply as The Conqueror, by 5 p.m.

The Conqueror takes "the box" on the ferry over to St. Thomas and hails a taxi for *The Daily News* plant in Charlotte Amalie, where they print *The Melee*.

The Conqueror gets drunk on Heinekens with the $20 bills the Publisher gives him. He sleeps it off at his sister's house and comes back on the ferry early Monday morning with about 3,000 weekly newspapers.

We haven't failed to get the paper out in 15 years, a record no one, including ourselves, can believe.

On Mondays I wake up, stumble down the hill from my bungalow and climb another flower drenched hill to the newspaper office. By the time I hop into the passenger seat of the rented jeep the Publisher has already begun talking. Plans for this, schemes for that, a constant stream of banter and greed-driven babble that I have come to enjoy spews from his thin bearded head.

I inspect the new paper, put a Phish tape in the cassette deck and the Publisher and I begin to wheedle and glide through Roach Harbor delivering our humble and sometimes horribly controversial product. The Publisher is named Caleb Barnegat. He talks with abandon, his privileged Massachusetts upbringing seeping out through every sentence. I count out bundles of 50 newspapers for the stores. A good issue sells out in two days and we restock on Thursday. We mail half of the three thousand papers stateside.

The Monday route is so familiar the Publisher can ramble on unceasingly about stories we must get to as we weave through the hungover streets.

The sun seems to always shine on St. Simon and I am prone to daydreams as the routine unfolds. Out the window of the jeep I hand free copies of the paper to security guards, taxi drivers, friends and anyone else interesting I see on the road.

My roots here are deep for a Continental. I was down from college visiting my folks when I first got involved in putting out this weekly paper. The Publisher liked my college training but was more interested in my ties to some of the first white people who claimed St. Simon for the hippie nation.

That was more years ago than I care to recite and now the hippies are into real estate and chain style gourmet restaurants. St. Simon has been discovered and sold many times over to a constant stream of tourists.

But it still has a certain charm.

Some days I wonder what I'm missing, tied to a tiny island, while my peers make their mark in the States. Most days, from the top of the island, I stare down the ancient pirate trail known as the Sir Francis Drake Channel and wonder why everyone else isn't in this beautiful place too.

Today the island is a fascinating study in micro-economics, self-indulgence, nature, the reserve of indigenous peoples and magic.

After you stay for a while you realize that the magic is a tangible part of the beauty.

When we got in the car this morning the Publisher was complaining that he didn't have any cash. It is his near constant mantra.

Leaving *The Melee* parking lot we lurched to a stop as an open-air "safari" taxi bus cut us off. Dressed in a loud Hawaiian style print shirt given to him by one of the local hotels, a giant black taxi man named Gumbs jumped out of his open air bus with a huge smile and approached our light green rental jeep. He put two one hundred dollar bills in the Publisher's open hand. It was an old debt I know nothing about. We were thanked for a Carnival preview that Gumbs had hoped would be in today's paper. We left him flipping through the new issue looking for something that didn't exist. The Publisher slipped me a hundred dollar bill and adroitly pulled out around Gumbs' bus. Caleb negotiated his way expertly back on to the left side of the road and we started our paper route. Bolstered by our apparent good fate, we proceeded with aplomb, two exiled idiots in paradise.

That kind of "St. Simon nice" magic happens all the time. I refuse to get sappy about this place because it is just another place. But I notice it when I'm hungry and out of the blue the neighbor arrives with a roast turkey left over from one of the island restaurants. You start thinking that you are hot and it rains for about 5 minutes.

Of course there is an all too apparent dark side to this paradise too. Especially since the airlines have made it easier to arrive and exploit this former outpost.

We wag our heads on the good days and hope that time freezes because St. Simon is really a tropical flower. It silently blooms in brilliant sunshine but then can only wither and die in the heat.

This particular Monday we take a business like approach to the paper route, hitting the irritable Miss Crabapple's news kiosk, Arno's Convenience Store, Starfruit Market and the drug store. Caleb begins his daily pot smoking ritual heading out of town on South Shore Road and neither of us mentions a story about deformed frogs that appeared in the Sunday Science section of the *New York Times* the previous day. We drop *The Melee* off at The Arab owned Peace Pipe Market where the locals shop and the Grand Hyatt resort where the tourists cavort. We sell some more papers at the Tropicale Superette and spot Hillary behind the deli counter.

"I've never seen you up before noon in my entire life," the Publisher tells the young barfly. I give her a paper and she can't suppress her 23 year-old smile.

Pale, titless, thin and hiding her baby dreadlocks under a golf cap, Hillary is adorable if only for the energy she radiates. A rare and beautiful bud threatening to bloom, she is probably bound for a stateside rehab center if she doesn't slow down.

We make jokes with Hillary about it snowing outside and continue to rib her about working the morning shift. She pretends to ignore us as we grab bottles of iced tea from the freezer.

Back in the rental jeep the Publisher ignites his first really big joint of the paper route on the winding roads of Contant on the way back to town. We enjoy the vistas of St. Thomas through the native yards and the Publisher relishes the dirty island weed.

This first "story meeting" of the day now behind us the conversation turns briefly to the existence of the article in yesterday's *Sunday New York Times* about deformed frogs. I've been obsessed with the increase in appearances of deformed frogs since witnessing a Bread and Puppet Theater play on the ominous subject during a vacation foray to Vermont in the early 1990's. It is subject I broach with the Publisher quite often, if only to warn him that the earth is a closed system and, according to the basic principles of science, specifically the Second Law of Thermodynamics, it is quite possible that the earth will run out of energy.

"Frogs prove this?" he usually counters, rolling his eyes. And I try to explain to him that yes, entropy affects frogs like everything else.

The Sunday *Times* is our main connection with the outside world on this Caribbean rock. About 20 Sunday *New York Times* usually arrive on the noon boat on Sundays. They are sold at Lucky's Liquor and Jewelry store in Roach Harbor for the lofty price of $13.50. The precious mainland paper is printed in Ft. Lauderdale, probably on Friday, but it is a coveted link for both the Publisher and myself, partially because we fancy ourselves journalists and partially because we often feel culturally marooned.

I could never pay $13.50 for a newspaper on sheer hobo principal. The Publisher, however, is an old money Yankee and doesn't even balk at the price.

Fortunately for me, an ugly incident involving Lucky's Liquor and Jewelry store arose a few years back when a start up monthly newspaper began competing for advertising dollars and space on the news rack with *The Melee*. The Publisher made a habit of going into Lucky's, picking up the entire pile of the free monthly newspapers and promptly hurling them in the trashcan in Roach Harbor Park.

A confrontation naturally ensued. Since that fabled incident transpired (which found the Publisher whacking a stately business woman from St. Louis with her own newspaper inside the gift shop after he was caught red handed) the Publisher hasn't been allowed to set foot in the store. I have adopted a Sunday routine of buying the paper for him and it is a routine, which for me, nearly rivals the next days paper route for sheer pleasure.

Usually around noon on Sunday, the Publisher peels off a Jackson from his wad of $20 bills and I walk down hill from *The Melee* office past the Esso and the Lester February School. I greet the well-dressed churchgoers with earnest "good mornings" and eventually I plunk the bill down on the glass counter at Lucky's.

I am suspect for my relationship to the Publisher at the store but I am also considered the least excitable staff member of the island newspaper. Sometimes I am even greeted with a smile. I take the Sunday Times from the rack and a Heineken from the freezer and put a $5 bill (my change) in my pocket. In seconds I have it spread out on a bench in Roach Harbor Park and spend a blissful couple hours or so with the coveted paper.

I have no television and no Internet. The radio is just for rock and roll or calypso. So this oasis with the Publisher's expensive paper is a hallowed ritual and necessary connection to my concept of reality.

When I am satiated, I fold the Times back as neatly as possible and bring it back up the hill to *The Melee*. The Publisher grabs it greedily from me, asks me where I have been and heads off to the beach with the paper, his girlfriend and his young son. He will complete the crossword in short order and read the headlines later.

I am left in peace to tweak that particular week's edition of *The Melee* to finality and hand it over to The Conqueror.

Again, it is a well-rehearsed dance.

This morning on the Roach Harbor section of our paper route we barely discussed yesterdays *Sunday Times* or the frog story. We've been saving it.

We have a 40 minute ride over two mountains ahead of us to Fort Bay, where we will deliver papers to the stores serving the small but tight knit West Indian population and the growing community of Continental boaters on that end of the island. Rumored to be the witness relocation capital of the world, Fort Bay does have a charming seediness to it that is not lost on the first time visitor.

After Fort Bay we will turn back and drive along St. Simon's beautiful North Shore dropping off newspapers at campground stores, yogurt stands and Rockefeller's hotel, before calling it a day in the early afternoon. It is clear to both Caleb (I just prefer to call him the Publisher), and myself, that idle chit-chat about the frog story will provide much of the entertainment for today's paper delivery, so neither of us attempts to rush the matter.

We pick up a cute hitchhiker who looks like a friend of Hillary's, just as we ease out on to Centerline Road. The Publisher lights another joint, but the hitchhiker isn't interested. She is nestled into the backseat next to the piles of *The Melee* and forgotten. The Publisher puffs and we pick up opposite sides of the debate over whether the abundance of deformed frogs reported in New England, Wisconsin and Minnesota has been caused by a hole in the ozone or by pockets of industrial pollution.

The boss goes into a lengthy soliloquy about how water borne deformities in frogs are a certain harbinger of trouble to come in the human womb, a hypothesis he ripped off from the *Times* article. Still it is fascinating when translated into his concise newspaper style parlance and I question him about the potential bellwether nature of the frog discoveries. We ramble on about the picture the *Times* had of a frog with a leg jutting out of its head and joke about the fossils the deformed frogs will make.

A half hour goes by before we realize the hitchhiker in the back seat is balling her eyes out, weeping steadily onto a pile of newspapers. The Publisher pulls the car over and we try to discern the reason for her tears.

It turns out this young woman is not a friend of Hillary's but a traveler recently arrived from France. She has very little English but is convinced the Publisher and I have been making fun of French people.

"The French people are not deformed frogs," she tells us through her tears.

Our apologies can simply not change the mind of this young creature. Her tears subside but she will not believe that we do not intend to run her over and leave her "frog fossil" to be picked at by Turkey Vultures.

After ten minutes we finally coax her back into the jeep and take her to Fatty Kegs, where she has a job interview to be a bar maid.

We finally leave her with a handful of *Melees*, one for her and some for the early bar flies at Fatty Kegs. We tell her to have Mark or Gerry, who own the bar, call us for our blanket recommendation.

Now seemingly pestered, the young French woman seems to snicker and sneer at us. Confused but not daunted the Publisher talks about doing a favorable story about the French when Bastille Day comes around. She dries her eyes, still really not sure if we are putting her on or not, and storms off.

I never know what to expect on paper route day.

chapter 3

Tuesday morning in the afternoon

O n Tuesday I try and get a few news stories done for
The Melee. Just to get a jump on things. But this morning I couldn't
get going. I ruled out a morning swim in Jumbala Bay. I didn't
want to see Jenny and I knew she would be there.

I should have got up and gone to work but instead I got up,
turned on a talk radio show on the local A.M. station and fell back
to sleep. Buzzing mosquitoes rustled me from my early morning
nap and I reached for my battery powered swatter and began frying
the pesky bugs in mid-air.

Shaped like a small tennis racquet, the electric swatter is an
ingenious device designed by a sick person. Two double A batteries
electrify the metal strings of this tennis racquet with a sharp charge.
The current is enough to sizzle a mosquito on contact.

This morning's bugs, the same offenders who were allowed to
run amok on my uncovered sleeping torso all through the previous
evening's deep sleep, were juicy with my blood. They sparked and
sizzled upon contact with the racquet, lighting up the room and
sizzling like frying red meat on a grill. It was such fun I swatted
flies for most of the morning, sweeping out a small pile of about
40 confirmed kills by around 11 a.m.

Due to this interlude I didn't make it down the hill to *The Melee* until nearly 1 p.m.

Fortunately anything that happens on a Tuesday is so old news by the next Monday there is little pressure to even show up to work. While it doesn't pay to do any real reporting it does help to get ahead on copy in case something more interesting than working on the paper comes up during the latter half of the week. On Tuesdays I like to lean back on a few stock St. Simon issues, stuff that might interest stateside readers but is so old hat for St. Simonians it is hardly worth reporting. My two favorite stock subjects are the cheesy development types who are always proposing some tacky version of a condominium Paradise equipped with a pool (and in one recent case an executive putting green) and the alarming onslaught of Chinese aliens being smuggled into the U.S. through St. Simon.

They are safe subjects. Everybody hates the developers. They are greedy scum and they are making the tropics ugly. They are also a good target because, unlike the politicians, they don't have the potential for any violent retaliation to some good-natured muckraking.

As far as the aliens go, everybody unilaterally feels bad for the multitudes of Chinese refugees who wash up here with wet clothes and wide-eyed dreams of freedom. They pay thousands of dollars to be smuggled to U.S. soil only to be shuttled through the government bureaucracy for the slim chance they might be granted political immunity. Even if they do negotiate the political situation they still are likely to be trapped by the same people who sponsored their flight from China who hope to sell them into bondage in places like the Garment District of New York. If these refugees do gain asylum and escape their sponsors/slave masters, their future is still in jeopardy.

I was justifiably indignant about the alien smuggling issue for months and tried hard to sell some of my stories to the mainland newspapers. But they balked. The Associated Press will call my landlady Judy in the middle of the night and ask her to walk down the hill and wake me up so they can put me on a news story if it effects someone with ties to their readership. But nobody will touch the aliens. The Hartford Courant called everyday for two weeks when a live-aboard boater from Connecticut appeared to have been killed and robbed of the cash he was going to use to buy a boat. He was related to some rich Yankees and they wanted copy and pictures immediately for their front page. Interestingly they still haven't touched the alien story. I can't seem to get any news outlets interested in buying stories about literally thousands of smuggled Chinese aliens over what has become America's last open border. So be it. I pretty much gave up.

This is what I did come up with for stories on Tuesday before retiring to the bush to relax and swap stories with my friend Fred.

Jambala Bay Beach Club faces high hurdles

By Don Hunger
Melee Staff

Beads of sweat welling up under his blonde toupee local real estate developer Trevor Hartwell denied that his proposed 52 unit luxury time-share project would have any effect whatsoever on the environment at a public meeting of the Coastal Zone Management Association this week.

"It will be an asset to Jumbala Bay," the Detroit born developer told CZM chairperson and current Mayor, Eustis Smith. "I want to give something back to the community with this project."

The special CZM hearing was called to discuss a last minute addition to the architectural drawings for the proposal, which includes a "Habitrail" escalator spanning from the planned mountaintop development to Jumbala Bay Beach.

Smith dismissed comment from approximately 50 locals gathered to voice opposition to the giant "state-of-the-art" air conditioned escalator, explaining that the

29

public comment portion of the official permitting process had been over for months.

Hartwell first began clear cutting portions of the Jumbala Bay mountainside for the 52 Unit Beach Club in 1986, but was stymied by Hurricane Hugo in 1989 and Hurricane Marilyn in 1995 as well as the dissolution of numerous funding sources. Hartwell Erection Limited Liability Company (HELL CO.) is the latest moniker for the thrice bankrupt development company, which Hartwell told CZM, has finally procured financing for the project through the Bank of Grosse Point.

"We want to break ground in June," Hartwell told the CZM. "We would appreciate an approval tonight."

Smith granted a verbal approval but attorneys for the anti-development Friends of Jumbala Bay Association argued that because only Smith and local attorney Claire Fattenuff were on hand, a quorum was not achieved and the meeting was illegal.

Exasperated that the six-member board had not achieved a quorum since the previous December, Smith scheduled a mandatory meeting of all CZM members for May 30. Smith had no comment about the agenda of that meeting when questioned by *The Melee.*

Members of Friends of Jumbala Bay gathered at the meeting complained of being muted by Smith and ambushed by Hartwell's "habitrail" proposal. They also grumbled about the lack of snacks or any liquid refreshments at the public meeting.

"Let's go to the Backyard and get tanked," commented one opponent to Hartwell's planned 52 unit Beach Club, a suggestion which effectively broke up the meeting.

Historical Society meets Aliens

by Don Hunger

Melee Staff

"Look at all these clothes, these people will sleep anywhere," commented Myrtle Benderz at this past Saturday's Historical Society field trip to the Glucksberg ruins.

Benderz was of course referring to the stereotypical "hippie" types that have washed up on St. Simon since the late 1960's. While the shortage of affordable housing does arguably encourage free spirits to live in the bush, it was not the case on this April morning. The garments strewn belonged to 31 aliens who landed on the beach near the ruins of the former Glucksberg sugar plantation. After an all night boat trip from St. Maarten, the Chinese nationals landed in neck deep water early Saturday, wading to U.S. soil near the Federally owned ruins of the former slave plantation.

The landing party included a dozen women with at least three small children, witnesses said.

Twenty-eight of the aliens, including two who purchased cigarettes at the Sugar Bay camp store, were detained by National Park officials and handed over to INS.

The clothing was still dripping wet from the aliens' pre-dawn plunge, when spotted by Myrtle Benderz and other Historical Society members who were on an educational walk around one of the many slave quarters that abutted the two century old sugar mill and rum factory.

One of the Historical Society members with a cell phone called Roach Harbor Relish Queen Hot Lips Lola and she sped out and collected the aliens' wet clothing for disbursement amongst her friends.

"I've got two satin jackets and two Michael Jordan t-shirts," Hot Lips told *The Melee*. "Most of the rest of the stuff is child sizes, come on down to the store, I can't wear any of it."

The alien arrival marked the fifth known landing in four months on St. Simon and brings the estimated year to date apprehended alien landing count to 107. Sources behind the bar at Fatty Kegs said it was still too early to say whose predictions looked the best in the watering holes "Guess the Alien Count" fund raiser. The winner of the annual lottery, aimed at starting a defense fund for the aliens, will receive a small Sony television and cell phone, the Tuesday morning bartender reminded *The Melee.*

Despite repeated warnings from National Park Officials and St. Simon Mayor Eustis Smith, there still have been no fines levied or charges brought for aiding and abetting any illegal aliens who might have gone undetected by local officials.

Smith had no comment on this particular influx of aliens.

Informed by *The Melee* that the clothes belonged to dripping aliens instead of hippies, Benderz only reiterated her request to remove her real estate company advertisements from *The Melee.*

chapter 4

Phred

I come for the stories. And, of course, for the companionship. Cartoon large blue eyes roll in acceptance, as Fred fingers a slice of a mango I just picked from his jungle yard and sliced up with my Swiss Army knife.

We are out in the bush. From the main road a steep dirt road winds downhill and becomes more of a hiking trail as it winds up again toward a locked gate. Unlocked the gate reveals a foot path through a jungle crowded with trash-picked treasures. The path leads to a living museum for the last remaining hippie.

Fred's museum home is built, partly in cooperation with Mother Nature, Robinson Crusoe style, employing two large turpentine trees. It is constructed from thick beams salvaged from the wreckage of hurricanes and boatloads of memories. The walls are strewn with block and tackle from long sunk schooners and smuggling ships. Bad art and hurricane lamps are everywhere, giant candles, Mardi Gras beads, a collection of colorful shirts and the assorted clap-trap of 30 years on St. Simon decorate this un-electrified museum. I feel like I am a million miles away from Roach Harbor and *The Melee*.

The mango sliced, I set my sights on a bucket of congealed floor wax, which I cut loose and slowly feed to a burning homemade candle in a metal bucket. In the gloaming the first Cuban tree frogs start to croak and Fred eggs them on.

"Rrrbiit, rrribbbit."

Fred is clearly amused with the idea of talking to the frogs and his eyes grow even wider, reflecting their seasoned madness in the candle light.

The frogs, mistakenly imported from Castro's Cuba by some researchers in the 1970's, take up Fred's gauntlet. We are met with a thunderous cacophony of croaks in the Caribbean night. I wonder aloud why you don't see deformed frogs in the Caribbean.

I go for the transistor radio to tune out the frogs. I pop two warmish Heinekens. No electricity means no fridge and ice melts too quick for it to be economical. Fred could have thousands of dollars buried on the property from various Caribbean adventures but he insists upon making do on beans and rice and maybe some booze if I bring some up to his museum.

I like to get out of Roach Harbor, which is full of noisy beach bars and sunburned tourists in the winter.

Tonight I'll camp out in the bush. Fred and I will watch the sky for satellites and rehash the business of the day.

The battery powered rock and roll radio brings us a nugget from the sixties and I coax Fred into one of his favorite stories of how he met Janis Joplin in St. Thomas well over thirty years ago. It is a story I love and I am continually astounded by the attention to detail in my friend's storytelling. At *The Melee*, I exaggerate the hell out of everything. In Fred's stories the details, I have learned first hand, never alter from the original event.

"I missed the last bus," Fred explained, talking about a night over thirty years ago like it was last week. "I was drinking in the waterfront bars and my boat was on the other side of the island in Red Hook. In those days there were no cars going that direction in the middle of the night and bars stayed open all night. It was about three in the morning so I had a few hours to kill before I could hitch a ride home."

Fred's hands began to move and his eyes re-widened as he

launched into this memoir. I easily picture his ghost of years ago sitting on a barstool in an empty Charlotte Amalie watering hole, sipping on a draft beer and waiting for the sun.

"She walked in and went right for the jukebox, it was only the bartender and I and maybe some other rummy in the whole place," Fred explained. "She found her song on the jukebox but she didn't play it, she played something else."

"She sat down next to me and ordered a shot of Southern Comfort. I was speechless, this was 1968 and Janis was a very big deal. I was trying hard to be cool and not to spook her.

"You look familiar," I told her.

"Oh yeah, well just who do you think I look like," Janis replied.

"Frank Zappa," I told her.

"Janis loved it," Fred explained. "She slapped me on the back and bought me a whiskey. Before I knew it she was gone, pushing her way out through the swinging doors just as fast as she came in, all of a sudden her music was playing on the jukebox."

"Word spread that Janis was on St. Thomas like wildfire," Fred explained. "Two days later this guy I knew was telling me all about it, I didn't let on that I had already seen her.

"He said Janis wanted to go for a sailboat ride, but she didn't want to go with just anyone, she wanted to go with someone who was cool. I told the guy I would take Janis out the next day.

At the time I had a nice wooden double ender, about 30 feet long, with beautiful lines. The boat didn't have an engine but I didn't really need one. It was a nice sailing boat.

"At the time I had a guy name Todd living on the boat with me, he was a real freak with hair down to his waist. He was a real lady's man too. I remember telling him we were going to take Janis out sailing and I know he didn't believe me."

"The day came and it was a little overcast and kind of blustery, it wasn't the best day but it was a good day for sailing. The morning went by and Janis never showed up, I kept telling Todd to watch the dock with the binoculars so he could row in and get Janis. He still thought I was kidding.

"She showed up around 3 p.m., with a whole entourage of record company hanger-ons. I was yelling to Todd that she was at the dock. When he finally saw her through the glasses his jaw dropped. It took Todd three trips to get Janis and all her groupies out to the boat. When Janis got on board she recognized me immediately.

"I should of known it would be you," she told me.

"They had all sorts of food, chips, dips, olives, booze, all sorts of stuff you couldn't get in the Virgin Islands at the time. We put up the sails and it was obvious that most of them had never been on a boat before.

"Janis was scared at first but after I explained to her the physics of the boat, the fact that the keel was so heavy it wouldn't allow us to tip over, she was much better. She just didn't want to tip over.

"Everybody else though, except Todd and myself, was terrified. We were slogging through some good chop, really sailing. Janis started to get into it and I let her hold the wheel. She took off her shirt and showed everybody her giant nipples.

"The record company crew was still gripped, however, a few of them, I think they had eaten some pills, probably Quaaludes, and were throwing up.

"After sailing for about twenty minutes I came about and explained that everybody who wanted to go ashore had one chance, one chance only. I was sailing for the beach and when I said jump they could get off or spend the rest of the afternoon on the boat. When I got to the beach most everybody jumped off. A few guys wanted to stay but Todd and I just started throwing them into the ocean. After we pried the grip of the last guy off the starboard stay, we chucked him in the water and turned out to sea, me, Todd and Janis.

"We slipped into a real nice reach and really started having fun, Janis loved sailing.

Todd got naked and asked Janis if she wanted some clam dip. He put his hand in the dip, grabbed a big handful and put it on the head of his prick.

"No thanks," Janis said. "But if you guys want to make love to me you can. You can do me after one of my shows. After I've made love to the whole audience for two hours, then you can do me."

Fred's wild eyes radiated when he got to that part, his smile betrayed just how vividly he remembered the day's event.

Fred went on to explain how he got to be friends with Janis over the next few weeks. He retold the story of listening to the first recording of her new album on the hotel room bed at Bluebeards Castle Hotel. He retold the story of having dinner with Janis and a friend at L' Escargot, which was at the time the best restaurant in the Caribbean.

"She was on junk," Fred remembered. "She wasn't interested in the food at all. I ate my meal and took hers and her friend's meal back to the boat in a bag. We had a few meals that ended that way."

Fred finishes this rock star story by retelling the very tempting invitation that resulted from his missed bus ride.

"Janis said, you're from New York, come up to Woodstock with me this summer, you can be my guest, I will fly you up there."

"I told her I had read in the paper that Woodstock wasn't going to happen, that they couldn't find a place for the concert."

"Janis said, 'Baby, I'm going to Woodstock this summer and so are a lot other people, you can bet that its going to happen."

"I had just bought the boat," Fred explained, slipping back into the present. "I didn't want to go back to New York. I had had enough of the whole trip."

So like time itself, Woodstock just sort of passed Fred by in the Caribbean. In his museum the cover from the very album that they listened to over three decades earlier is still tacked to a wall. In the photograph you can see through Janis's oversized spectacles and look into her equally wide eyes. When you stare at the picture closely you can't help but think it could be Fred's lost sister.

The album cover is faded and wilting, but her wide eyes are still clear behind the Hollywood glasses.

Down Island

chapter 5

Office Politics

I usually love a parade.

That's how my work gets done. People parade into the newspaper office, they are usually angry about something or someone or they are looking for publicity.

I take out my notepad, let them vent, jot down a few notes, maybe snap a few photos and then send them on their way. By Friday I can fill the paper with the complaints of irate snowbirds, the comings and goings of developers and business owners, gossip and the accomplishments of an occasional sixth grader.

This morning, however, just as I'm about to snuggle into coffee and a cranberry muffin from Rodney's Bakery, I see the physically impressive Mayor of St. Simon standing larger than life at the door of *The Melee*. I open the door just as the Mayor is about to rap his huge hand on the door. He nearly whacks me but is too flustered to apologize as he stumbles into our tiny two-desk four chair, newsroom. He collects himself and halfway into an apology for tapping me on the shoulder he begins yelling at me about a news story in *The Melee*.

In the space behind the newsroom the Publisher lives with his young son and girlfriend in a connected one-bedroom apartment that affords little privacy or separation from the daily business of *The Melee*.

Eustis Smith now dominates the newsroom with his large frame and an intensely bothered look in his ivory white eyes. I am hoping that his indecipherable rant will get the Publisher out of bed and put him between me and this excited Mayor.

"Who do think you are, you can't just write whatever you want in *The Melee*," the Mayor is telling me as the sleepy-eyed Caleb peeks in from his kitchen.

I apologize for calling him over the weekend, on a Saturday morning, and try to explain that we interpreted his hanging up on me as a "no comment."

Of course I mentioned in most every news story in the last issue, including the one about the sixth grader from the Dominican Republic whose parents and teachers are thrilled that she is reading English after only eight weeks in local schools, that St. Simon Mayor Eustis Smith had "no comment."

In fact the only story we didn't mention that the Mayor had "no comment" had to do with a trash problem which I am learning he is very sensitive about.

It seems a large clique of white people in the expensive Botnay Bay neighborhood got sick of their trash not being picked up at the dumpster drop off sites so they took up collections and gave the money to Mayor Smith to replace the small 30 year old dumpsters with some newer models. This way the trash wouldn't constantly overflow and attract rodents and trash pickers.

Smith got right on it and negotiated the purchase of these beautiful blue trash bins for the entire island. He put the first ones to arrive in Botnay Bay a month ago much to the delight of the wealthy snowbirds who coughed up a good sum for the larger dumpsters. A week later the Department of Public Works figured out that the winches on their garbage trucks were not capable of lifting up the dumpsters to empty them into their trucks.

The trash has sat marooned in the new receptacles on the side of the road in Botnay Bay in a growing pile ever since. The white people in the neighborhood have been steaming about their donation and cursing the Mayor as they all heave even more daily household trash on the overflowing mounds of trash which now dwarf the shiny new blue dumpsters. The Publisher took lots of pictures of that with his disposable camera and made a photo collage of the big mess on page 3 in this past week's paper.

"We are going to call that trash pile in Botnay Bay 'Eustis Smith Mountain,'" Caleb tells the ticking time bomb that the Mayor has become since his gubernatorial appointment.

Mayor Smith's eyes get even whiter hot and he looks at the Publisher in disbelief that he would dare mock him on what has obviously become a very sensitive issue.

I apologize again for bothering him at home about the logistics of the trash problem.

"I really don't think you are sorry," the long, thick, very black and physically imposing Mayor is telling me.

Eustis Smith garnered his coveted Territorial government job from the governor in return for campaign support. He is still not used to the media.

"He shouldn't apologize, he kissed your ass," the Publisher screams at Smith, pointing at me.

Every issue is a little more complex than it might seem on St. Simon. Every news story peels another layer off a giant onion of West Indian family ties and connections. I am personally frightened of Eustis Smith and decide not to open my mouth.

"Who does this cracker think he is, he just walks into meetings in my office without the courtesy of saying good morning," the Mayor screams.

"Did you just call my reporter a cracker?," Caleb asks the Mayor in horror.

It goes on from here and gets much worse, which would be fine if the Mayor wasn't related to everybody and anybody of any authority on the island. He climbed up the chain of command without ever leaving St. Simon, a rare feat reserved only for the politically astute.

Smith joined the Department of Public Works after high school and because he was bright and loyal but mostly because he showed up for work he was appointed island Director of the DPW on his fortieth birthday. On his 45th birthday the new governor in St. Thomas saw an ally for life and appointed him Mayor.

There is much conjecture that the Mayor is actually an illegitimate child of the governor but that is just grist for the cocktail hour gossip mill. Most discount the theory because the governor is widely known to be homosexual. Still, many islanders point out, both politicians are six feet four inches tall. And they both have astoundingly long fingers, I notice again, as Mr. Smith violently points at me.

Interestingly, St. Simon was the site of the first successful slave revolt in the Western Hemisphere. Termed an insurrection by scholars, it occurred in 1733 and the slaves held the island for over six months. The remaining holdouts from the French soldiers enlisted to take back the island killed themselves under a Lignumvitae tree instead of surrendering. It is a history that many of the locals are justifiably very proud of.

The original families living on St. Simon before the emergence of tourism were some of the only native people in the Caribbean to actually profit from the rapid gentrification of their tropical paradise. Most West Indian natives are graceful and genteel. On St. Simon many have also been smart enough to hold on to their valuable land and heritage.

Their offspring, who inherited this island largely cordoned off by a National Park (which is run from Atlanta and attracts the multitudes from the Northeast with money literally falling out of their pockets every winter), are sometimes less gracious. Many natives justifiably hold grudges against the increased pace in which time on St. Simon marches on.

At times Eustis Smith can be one of those bitter natives. On the outside he is a fastidious public official, one who often chimes up in public meetings about how a person's skin color doesn't matter to him. Privately he calls me a cracker. Somehow though I trust his heart is in the right place. The Publisher disagrees.

The momentum of the Mayor's rant about the muckraking ways of *The Melee* is partly interrupted when a small fat interior designer named George walks into the tiny newsroom with a tape measure. The Publisher and his young girlfriend have agreed to an absurd deal with George in which he will build us a "modern looking" office in his spare time, replacing our tired tables which are propped on filing cabinets and stacks of old newspapers with a more "modern" approach.

In return for his finish carpentry George, a slick émigré' from NYC, gets a lifetime of free advertising for his business card size advertisement.

"They don't call these winds outside the Trade Winds for nothing," some of our more savvy clients often joke with the Publisher.

I personally benefit greatly from the trades and eat at restaurants that advertise for free and sign for groceries at markets that have ads. The Publisher has three massage therapists advertising in the paper. None of them pays cash for their ads and the tiny staff stays very limber.

George negotiates his way around the screaming official's flailing arms, spreading out his tape measure here and there, like the angry black giant is invisible. In frustration the Mayor finally storms out. Before he leaves I'm threatened with a lawsuit and a beating.

He scares the shit out of me.

Down Island

chapter 6

Dr. Robert

The morning ritual of coffee, muffin and a visit to the Publisher's commode, which happily includes the thorough investigation of the piles of Vanity Fair and W magazines next to the toilet, was further delayed when a short-haired, serious-looking stateside fellow knocked on the door.

The Publisher wouldn't go near the door when this guy knocked. Instead he called me out from the bathroom and hid behind the curtain which separates the newsroom from his kitchen.

The man at the office door had a briefcase in his hand and a business like look behind his serious glasses. Chances were, Caleb surmised, he had a summons.

"Good afternoon, Welcome to the *St. Simon Times*," I said to the man, purposely using the name of the other St. Simon newspaper to confuse him.

"I thought this was *The Melee*," he said to me handing me his card.

"Ben Thayer," the card announced. "Biographer."

I knew instinctively he came to talk about Robert Oppenheimer, the father of the Atomic Bomb.

While celebrities of many sorts have washed up on St. Simon, Oppenheimer was one of the few who really tried to make it home.

His mark became an indelible paradox on the island. His legacy is tangible beneath the swaying palms on the quiet Jumbala Bay beachfront where he would take his morning walks.

His friends described the gaunt man with a pipe as bird like, gentle and apologetic. He died a troubled and sad man after finding an interim peace on St. Simon. His wife Kitty openly drank herself to death, his daughter hanged herself near the beach where her father once walked, pondering physics.

"I came to see if I could talk to anyone who knew the Oppenheimer family," the man said politely.

"I am a biographer."

"Did you bring any beer?" I asked him.

He looked at me quizzically and then smiled.

"So are you getting any pussy here on St. Simon," Caleb said, emerging from hiding.

Thayer knew it was going downhill from here fast. The Biographer's smile and tolerance for sarcasm eventually won us over and we gave him a file to look at. He wouldn't get much more than curious public records from the manila file.

After vacationing at a St. Simon guest house in nearby Sugar Bay for years, Oppenheimer finally bought his beachfront land in the mid 1950's from a former Samoan King and his wife. The King, whose real name nobody could ever pronounce, fled Samoa with his Queen and a literal King's ransom during World War II.

Because of their immense size, the King was nearly 7 feet tall, the Samoans were called the "Gigantics" by the 700 or so St. Simonians who inhabited the island when they arrived in the early 1940's. They were respected and liked by the native population, but feared as well. The King and Queen lived in isolation on Jumbala Bay and the couple kept very much to themselves. They eschewed modern conveniences, which began arriving on St. Simon in the 1950's. They never took a television or a telephone. The only problem was taxes.

While the Gigantics, which was the actual name on their tax bill, brought copious amounts of their small country's fortune to St. Simon, the taxes on beachfront property were growing out of control and their finances began to dwindle.

It was Robert Oppenheimer who convinced King Gigantic to sell him a third of Jumbala Bay so the Gigantics could set up a trust for their only son, who they named Superman, after the comic book hero.

The trust would successfully defer taxes for many years.

The money from the sale also allowed the King and the Queen to indulge in luxury appliances, including a refrigerator. Friends of the King still describe the giant Samoan's utter amazement at the ice cube.

Oppenheimer built a more modern home in Jumbala Bay and the population of St. Simon watched as sadness slowly killed the scientist's family.

When Oppenheimer's daughter accepted the old man's murderous burden and hung herself from a tree on Superman Gigantic's family beach in the 1970's, she left a will. In the will she left her inheritance to the "People of St. Simon."

The local government, which had now become savvy to the value of land near Laurance Rockefeller's elegant hotel and the popular National Park, seized on the note immediately. They took control of Oppenheimer's third of the beach, installed a tacky pavilion and a contentious land dispute was underway. Superman, the National Park Service and the Virgin Islands government all lay claim to the beachfront. In recent decades private developers have jumped in and proposed plans to develop the hillside above the beach, land which everyone, including Superman and the local government thought was the property of the National Park.

The land, in fact, belonged to a "Friends Group" of the National Park. The "Friends Group" acquired the land through a trade with a native family in the 1980's and shortly after they got it, "The Friends" turned around and sold it to a stateside development team for millions.

Plagued by bankruptcies brought on by the astronomical purchase price and two destructive hurricanes, a long list of potential developers of the so called Jumbala Bay Club, all people connected to Trevor Hartwell, have failed miserably.

Conjecture over the development annually becomes ripe like fruit on the trees. Talk about the project swells. The project, many say, is not unlike the papayas Superman grafts and grows on the hillside. The plans to develop Jumbala Bay are often crushed but they never die, much the way that Superman's weighty papayas often ripen fat, fall to the ground and smash, only to bloom again.

Uncannily, something astounding from a natural disaster to a political fire-fight has always happened in the nick of time and the Jumbala Bay development seemingly disappears. But only briefly, until some more money is infused.

Both the Publisher and I doubt that the Biographer cares anything about this local lore. The history of Jumbala Bay and its potential development is St. Simon legend told over and over in the bars on the beaches and sunset verandahs of the island. It rarely plays anywhere else, so we give Thayer the entire file.

"I would really like to speak with someone who knew the Oppenheimers," Thayer tells us.

My 95 year old neighbor Golf Cart Judy and her late husband were one of the scientist's first and best friends. But Judy is a writer herself and could probably do a better job on a biography than Thayer so I keep quiet.

"Have you met Superman?" Caleb asks.

Before the Biographer can answer there is a knock on the door and it opens immediately after the rap. It is Superman's wife Amy. This Nubian beauty has a reputation for volatility and her eyes immediately fire darts at Thayer.

We realize he must have already been shooed from her beachfront home and we wonder why she is here.

Recoiled from the steely-eyed assault from Amy Gigantic, Thayer cowered in the corner of the office holding his manila file. We waited for him to speak but Amy interrupted.

"It's okay, those are public records," she told Thayer, "but," and now the Publisher and I received her shooting glance, "I guess I know who my friends are."

I felt like shit.

Superman was my friend. I didn't know Amy well but I admired her. She kept the giant Samoan wonder out of trouble.

And trouble was always looking for this wealthy, handsome, child of the St. Simon jungle. At six and a half feet he really was the picture of Tarzan. And the shoe (or lack thereof) fit too, despite the encroachment of cell phone toting lawyers, real estate agents, developers and corrupt government officials, Superman managed a relatively peaceful existence on his beach, in all his disheveled glory.

Right now he is probably the only man on St. Simon with land worth over $5 million dollars that uses an outhouse. He and Amy live comfortably in a six by eight foot air-conditioned shack, with a television so Superman can watch basketball games.

Nestled beneath the coconut palms in the sunset corner of Jumbala Bay, his shack sits on the prettiest little beach on St. Simon.

People will tell you Superman has a heart of gold and Amy the heart of a pit bull. I don't believe it. She is just the one charged with protecting the precious National Park in-holding, from the developers. Superman, his friends will tell you, could easily give it away like an extra aloe plant in his garden.

Both the Publisher and I could tell that Amy definitely had something on her mind the minute she came into the newsroom.

Initially the Biographer de-fused it. Thayer had the courtesy to excuse himself and Amy sat down and I got her some coffee.

I supposed that her visit had something to do with developer Trevor Hartwell. The local shark had his teeth sunk in the proposed development of the hillside above her home for many years now, and despite recent setbacks the project was generally gaining steam. Hartwell, it seemed, was gaining favor of the local legislature, so much so he nearly pushed plans for the "habitrail" escalator past the Coastal Zone Management board.

Almost immediately after Thayer left, George reappeared with his tape measure. He began to regale Amy with a vivid reenactment of the chewing out that the Publisher and I had just received from the Mayor, successfully deflecting her reason for coming in to the newsroom until another day.

Outside a mini-monsoon had begun whipping up, sheets of

rain dropping like heavy curtains from the heavens and washing clean the dusty streets of Roach Harbor.

Amy, it appeared, decided to hold her tongue and just listen to George go on and on about our verbal lashing. She clearly was enjoying it as a few more people found their way into the newsroom to get out of the sudden rain. Happily George reprised his story of the angry Mayor for them as well. The Biographer returned and was now becoming quite amused by the whole scenario. He started asking a lot of funny questions about how much work actually got done at the newspaper and that was all the Publisher needed.

"OUT," he screamed. "Everybody go home. We are not going to get anything done now."

The Publisher escorted us all out and locked the office, even to George and his tape measure.

I am usually quite happy to throw in the towel the moment somebody threatens me. I have never really cared to cause too much trouble on St. Simon despite my continued employment by the island's number one muckraker.

Amy said she was headed home, so I asked for a ride to Superman's Beach. The five minute onslaught of pelting rain now over, the streets were still pocked with puddles when we got to her car. Steam rose briskly from pavement in the re-emerging late morning sun giving Roach Harbor a very sultry and tropical feel. We hopped in Amy's late model SUV and rolled out of town, listening to the rock and roll radio. My worries slipped out the open windows as the car cut through the steam.

On the way out of town, unsolicited, Amy broke the friendly silence in the car.

"St. Simon is only as serious as you want it to be," she told me.

chapter 7

The Fiddler

Many people on St. Simon don't know the name Dick Doherty, even though they have danced nearly naked in front of him. The short bald man with the infectious grin is simply known as "The Fiddler."

Every winter a circus of nudity, recreational drugs and impassioned frivolity follow this free spirit around the Caribbean like a circus troupe. The Fiddler's appearance at local bars is usually announced a day or so in advance on paper signs tacked to tamarind trees. Hundreds of live-aboard sailors and sketchy white people show up for the music and the scene. He is feared, admired, followed and adored.

Amy negotiates the steep drive down to her and Superman's beach house and we pass Bullet Head Bill's big white van. Bullet Head is The Fiddler's number one roadie. We both saw trouble in the forecast.

"This can't happen today," Amy says to me with a very tired expression.

I smiled as we approached Superman's modest beach shack. About a dozen friends and hangers on surround a small table in the front yard playing music. Superman is at the center of it all, dressed in striped T-shirt. His long sun bleached hair is in his eyes and a large smile decorates his face. His big frame makes his Gibson guitar look more like a ukulele.

A 30-year old muscle-bound towhead we call Stoned Mason Stuart plays chords on his guitar while Superman inlays some offbeat but interesting leads. A Rastafarian with a giant head of hair stuffed into a tube-like cap keeps order on bongos. Fred has his tambourines out. But it is The Fiddler himself driving the train, jumping from note to note, extrapolating new melodies and turning old songs into older songs.

"Don't take the brown acid," The Fiddler says by way of greeting Amy and me. Then The Fiddler wipes his forehead with his elbow and bends his bow into his ancient axe. His pick-up band catches the signal and launches on cue into a song about a beer drinking pig.

Amy unsuccessfully tries to get Superman's attention and free him from The Fiddler's infectious momentum.

I grabbed a Heineken from the Honor Bar set up for the occasion, savor its chill in the warm sun and walk slowly into the Caribbean Sea, delighting in the contrasts of hot and cold.

A young boy and his mother are the only people on the pristine beach. They are playing on a tiny surf board in front of the house where the young Oppenheimer girl hung herself 25 years earlier.

It feels good to swim and I push on without looking. Eventually I almost beach myself on the white sand of Jumbie Beach at the other end of Jumbala Bay.

"I see a familiar face," a dark face with a cheery voice says to me. It is Horace Challenger, soaking in the sea after a busy morning driving taxi between Roach Harbor and the Hyatt. Mr. Challenger is telling a European man named Oskar a familiar and touching story he tells everyone he meets at the beach.

I wave to them both and listen as he tells Oskar about his first wife, Ethylene, and how she refuses to enjoy life. Mr. Challenger divorced Ethylene, giving up his house and car, to toil in Gumbs' taxi every day just so he could marry a childhood crush named Elizabeth January.

"Every day I was married to my Elizabeth was a joy to be alive," Challenger is telling Oskar.

One day while Challenger was driving taxi his new wife had a stroke. He called home to check on her but she couldn't answer the phone, she could just hear its ring and know her husband was calling.

When Challenger returned home that day Elizabeth was in bad shape. He took her immediately to the clinic in the middle of the island. The doctors at the clinic insisted she be shipped immediately to St. Thomas on the hospital boat.

Meanwhile Hurricane Marilyn was beginning to bear down on the island. The ambulance boat got Elizabeth to St. Thomas but when Mr. Challenger tried to follow he found the ferries were all shut down to prepare for the impending hurricane.

Challenger went home and called St. Thomas Hospital and reached a niece who worked as a nurse. She found a telephone and put it next to Elizabeth's ear. While the winds howled Mr. Challenger told Elizabeth over and over how much he loved her. He talked for hours until the telephone service was finally interrupted by the 140 mile an hour winds. His niece told him days later that his wife died with a smile on her face and the phone next to her ear.

Challenger lost everything in the hurricane and was forced to move back in with his first wife.

"I haven't seen her smile in years," Challenger was telling Oskar. "There is no joy in that woman's life. There is no justice in this world."

I wondered about that as I swam back to Superman's Beach. The size of the party had tripled in the hour and a half it took me to slowly swim to the other corner of Jambala Bay and back.

On my return I met Fred on the beach and he told me the beans were done. One giant restaurant pot was, in fact, filled with Fred's beans. Amy must of said if you can't beat them....because she made some rice and put out the paper plates and plastic forks.

A beautiful Caribbean day had bloomed from an ugly fight.

We drank and sang all day. We ate, some of us soaked in the sea, most everyone smoked and smiled. At dusk Fred and Stoned Mason Stuart built a fire from the dead mangrove trees in a swamp. The sun set over St. Thomas and we watched the electric lights begin to dot the island across the sound, something we had all done so many times before. In the gloaming the beach became our own very small world.

The Fiddler had a paying gig in Roach Harbor and the party followed him there. We sat by the fire and Superman and Stuart, still sober, sang the favorite song from the daylong party… "The storm is lifting…We got the moon and stars above…"

Later the giant islander named Superman told me what had excited his wife earlier that morning which now seemed so far away.

National Park Rangers, the St. Simonian explained, had arrived shortly after 8 a.m. that day. They woke him up and informed him he must move his mooring ball and mooring from the ocean floor in front of his beach. Superman keeps a Boston Whaler on the mooring for fishing trips and joy rides. His father, the Samoan King dropped an old engine block for the mooring before the National Park arrived in 1956.

Superman isn't used to arguing. He tried to reason with the Rangers but they were just hacks from the Federal government, not St. Simonians, who would consider a situation and make up their own minds. Reasoning with the stateside park people never goes well. Superman said he called his lawyers, which is disheartening to hear. A nature boy like Superman, a man who rides his horse to town, drinks rum from the bottle and swaggers like a western gunslinger, a man who grew up on the branches of this island's beautiful genip trees, shouldn't have to live in a world of cell phones and lawyers.

But what really worried Amy was that Superman and his cohorts would take matters into their own hands.

The National Park in conjunction with the Virgin Islands government, at considerable expense, installed about 200 moorings in the bays around St. Simon to revive the bare-boat charter business, which had been slowly usurped by the more pristine British Virgin Islands in recent years. The local government's plan was to get the boats back with free moorings, make the business people happy and then begin charging the rich yachties $30 a night for the moorings. The planned revenue from the mooring balls had probably already feathered the nest I suspected Eustis Smith was building. He was the first to sign off on the plan.

But this morning in a sleepy rage, Superman as much as told the low level Rangers dispatched to hassle him that if his mooring had to go, their moorings did too.

In the fire's light I saw the gleam from Stoned Mason Stuart's sharpened machete. A pirate's smile was plastered across his face. Amy had already given up and gone to bed. Fred had put his tambourines away and was getting ready for a boat ride.

I took one more slug of rum and decided to walk home by myself. A two-mile walk in the Caribbean night is often a beautiful thing, but this was more of a stagger. Still I made a mental note to myself to get up early and put some film in the camera.

It would be a spectacular news photo to capture 200 new National Park mooring balls idly floating down the Sir Francis Drake Channel with the sun rising to push them along. I could almost hear The Fiddler singing a bluegrass tune about the mystery of the missing mooring balls.

Only Superman, The Fiddler would sing, could have big enough mooring balls for this sort of thing.

Down Island

chapter 8

Island Rhythm

St. Simon spiderwebs
have beads of
precipitation
bending each line

seasons slip
through the matrix
leaving only the
water behind.

Rhythm is everything on St. Simon.

It is the key to the symphony of happiness you see on the familiar island faces. You see it on the natives, people like Superman, who flow with the rhythm of nature and allow you a glimpse at the machinations of time. You see it on the faces of the children who don't know the worry mainland children learn too quickly.

You watch the tourists being shuttled into safari busses and herded off to beaches and back on to cruise ships and you appreciate time. In the future time will be worth more than money and free time will be non-existent. St. Simonians, of course, will transcend this and they will find a way to escape the increasing cost of time.

"They are never going to miss us," Almando Smith, a relative of

57

the Mayor, told me this morning from the roadside perch where he sells plants and carves lignumvitae wood. A lot of people like me are hiding out for the time being on St. Simon, passing time, drinking too much. But others have escaped permanently. Others still, like the Publisher, unfortunately can't seem to leave the rest of the world alone.

It's funny to watch Caleb try to function on both clocks, Continental time and Island time. He straddles the crevasse with his bony legs as if each were fastened to skis moving slowly apart from each other. He will get to the beach, take his clothes off, breathe in and then call one of his lawyers on his cell phone.

It is equally sad to watch Eustis Smith try to speed up time with his maladroit efforts to erase impossible infrastructure dilemmas. While duct tape and Band-aid approaches fixed problems in the Caribbean for years, they are only one finger in a big dam holding back a reservoir swelling with time.

"Small island has big problems," Almando tells me, trying to sum up the situation.

Yes, (and tourists ask me this all the time) the people on St. Simon do move slowly. But time doesn't. It just moves differently than other places.

Instead of steadily progressing in an orderly fashion with normal gradations, time wells up like a summer storm on St. Simon. It slow boils then explodes. Nothing will happen for months and then everything will happen at once. Then, the next morning everything and nothing will be the same. Much the way the Sept. 11 attack changed time, events on St. Simon are recorded in the mental inventories of the residents and used as benchmarks.

People in St. Simon relate to numerous time-space realities.

For many of the older folks there was the time before the tourists. These were the days when only a few white pioneers like Golf Cart Judy, her Russian husband and Superman's parents were some of the only Continentals on St. Simon. It was the 1950's and time was abundant, everybody pitched in and made do. When there was a party everyone was invited.

Like anyplace the "old days" are hashed over like a golden age on St. Simon. The "old days' are so coveted, in fact, a unique pecking order of superiority seems to relate more to how long a person has been on St. Simon as opposed to what they have done since they arrived. Native status is akin to membership in an elite fraternity.

In the old days brilliant old men danced with cans of Old Milwaukee beer on their heads in the shadow of the rickety wooden Customs building in Roach Harbor Park. Everybody was friendly and many St. Simonians, God bless them, rekindle these harmonic days in small ways every day.

Unfortunately it is widely considered fact that everything has gone slowly and steadily downhill since electricity, telephones and cars became commonplace.

In the 1970's St. Simon entered the new destination years. The number of people who discovered the island began to increase exponentially. The hippies arrived and brought marijuana, rock and roll music and eventually greed. Finally one hotel wasn't big enough and the Hyatt was built out by Great Roach Harbor. The lure of sex, drugs, and the promise of big money brought some interesting and unscrupulous characters to the Caribbean in both the 1970's and the 1980's.

Then there were the hurricanes. Only the strong survived the material and mental damage wrought by Hugo in 1989. It wreaked physical and emotional havoc. One day you had a house, the next day it was in the neighbors yard. Then came Marilyn in 1995. This blow was not quite the destructive force that Hugo was, but in many ways it made people edgier. It made islanders wary of becoming attached to personal possessions and to some extent to other people. In some ways the storm fueled theories that the islands were a modern day Sodom and Gomorrah. Before Hugo, hurricanes hadn't bothered the islands in half a century, a generation was raised without seeing their destruction.

The storms became how islanders measured time. Things happened "before Hugo," or someone arrived "just after Marilyn."

Invariably every story told by somebody who lives on St. Simon to any recent arrival ends up with two or more people out in the yard with the homeowner pointing into the distance and describing where something landed after the big blow. The stories almost always are punctuated by one local recalling how he saw something scream by in the wind during a storm. The stories usually end by describing the inspection of the wreckage the day after the storm and how they stood in the yard with the neighbors in front of some tangle of wood and corrugated metal and looked to each other, shrugged and said to each other, "Nope, that's not my roof."

Time, of course, continues to proceed with tricks of light and space in modern day St. Simon. While the threat of the strain of development from another luxury hotel lingers in the air, nothing happens. While Eustis Smith echoes the governor's promises of a new commercial port, a new post office and a new sewer system, nothing happens. Behind the scenes, however, wheels are turning. The anticipated tax dollars and pay-offs from Trevor Hartwell's proposed development are not even secretly being divided between private interests and plans for public improvements. One day something will happen and in the morning everything and nothing will have changed, for all of St. Simon.

For most residents who have adopted St. Simon, the non-linear approach to time has become essential. The United States is increasingly viewed as a large traffic jam with unpredictable results. The ugly tourists who arrive make us more wary. When a popular St. Simon couple were shot in a carjacking in Atlanta in the spring of 2001, many locals vowed never to leave their adopted island home, not even for a vacation during hurricane season.

My internal clock is constantly losing time to this complicated abyss. How could I ever leave this magical island for the real world. If I leave a destructive bureaucratic tangle of taxes and impossible heating bills must surely be around the bend. But if I stay I will surely become a certified crazy person with no hope of ever existing in that place they call the real world.

It's more complicated than the feeling of paranoia associated with having too much fun or too much of a good thing. But it's not too far from that either.

chapter 9

Marking Time

*E*arlier on this lovely Thursday afternoon the Publisher told me he "marks time" by the creation of human life. The comment ruined my day.

It bothered me so much that now I'm next door to *The Melee* office, sitting in front of a Heineken on a thick wooden stool at the Green Tree Inn's bar, still trying to swallow his remarks.

Stories about the Publisher's quirkiness, flagrant ganja habit and general malfeasance have been the subject of cocktail talk on this small Caribbean island since he arrived to edit his father's newspaper in 1980's. I have always fancied the idea that I knew him a little better than the rabble. I have always thought I had an insight into the pride he took in publishing a weekly newspaper. As foreign to me as it remains, I have continued to rationalize the expense of the fun he has publishing on a parental inheritance. But now despite my hope and faith, right now, in the neon twilight of these beer signs, I can't help but think he is completely screwed up.

In hjs salad days the Publisher had his kids and his wife Pam here.

They never adjusted, of course, because St. Simon is really a place for its natives. Wanderers and warriors, poets and pirates also seem to find peace on St. Simon, but not people from away who seek a decent suburban life. An Indian mystic once told me that St. Simon is very similar to sacred Indian land. You visit this land and celebrate its beauty to clear your head and make peace with your spirit. But you don't move to St. Simon permanently, it's hallowed ground.

Everybody certainly gave the Publisher's family credit for trying to blend into island life.

The Publisher always seemed to be able to hold it all together, even in his most stoned moments. Until recently he kept a home with his wife Pam in Cohasset Massachusetts. He commuted back to St. Simon, even in the summer, to put out the paper on Mondays.

In my nearly 15 years with the Publisher we have never failed to publish on Monday. I mention this again because I am truly astounded by it. Most everyone thought someone would either kill him or scare him to death and he would flee. There have been days when I personally was prepared to call in the men in white coats with their straight jackets to take Caleb away. Instead the threats the Publisher receives and the tangles he gets himself into make for good copy and somehow seem to fuel him. His eccentricities somehow seem to bolster his legend. *The Melee* prides itself on its consistency.

Eventually and in the name of everything decent, the Publisher's wife put her foot down and insisted Caleb come back to Cohasset, for good. He, of course, and partially in the name of everything depraved, stayed on St. Simon. The result is a fully blossomed three year love affair with a now 22 year old Israeli woman. A young son, Jared Barnegat, became the progeny of this odd union. Divorce proceedings have been on the Publisher's "to do" list for two years now.

The Publisher gets a lot of flack from people about this but not from me. Caleb is very proud of this new son and carries him around Roach Harbor like he birthed him personally. His love for his son and his girlfriend transcends any judgment.

"Don't even talk to me about that man," a thirty-plus something year old woman sitting next to me at the bar says. "Everybody hates him."

She of course doesn't know him at all. She says her name is Elise and she is wearing an absurd flower patterned dress over a hard body and drinking white wine and smoking cigarettes with abandon. She rails on about the negative stories and fact-less tomes we have published in the paper over the past few years since she moved here.

I have never met her and she doesn't realize I work at the newspaper. I am delighted with my anonymity, a very rare thing on this small island.

Her bluster is well rehearsed. Elise is a good bar talker.

The Publisher, of course, realizes that a growing number of residents of this transient community, especially the newer ones who haven't given up the booze yet, have a very skewed opinion of his infidelities and his controversial newspaper.

It is true, even in the Caribbean, that you cannot publish a decent news story without stepping on somebody's toes.

For the most part the Publisher doesn't care what the new people think, especially the white people like Elise who have recently arrived. They will be gone soon. A hurricane will spook them or the strange rock fever of living the life of an American ex-pat will move them home. That is the Publisher's philosophy.

Caleb's smart. He knows his bread is buttered by the native population and the hard core hippie settlers who first found St. Simon for the white people and dug in. A lot of them, some of my people, dug in tight enough to become successful without really trying. Some of these people even appreciate the Publisher's bawdy consistency. A few who care to think about it realize that we all take turns having our toes stepped on in the press.

I won't waste my hope and slightly shattered trust on Elise, I prefer to let her talk about the writing career she abandoned to sell timeshares for the Hyatt.

She asks me who I read and I pause like I haven't been asked this question by a hundred tourists.

"Richard Ford, Raymond Carver and Richard Brautigan," I tell her.

"All men," she says indignantly.

I nod as she launches into a forgettable sermon about Alice Munroe.

Before I know it I'm defending Stephen King as a representative of the male species and she is negotiating the purchase of a large bottle of white wine before the small hotel bar closes up for the night.

I'm still troubled by the remarks of the Publisher, but I'm just not ready to let my concerns spill out to this increasingly attractive barfly as I settle behind another greenie.

In his weaker moments, like today when he sprung this "marking time" thing on me, I wonder how comfortable the Publisher is with his new family.

"Babies are how people mark the passing of time," were his exact words. It was just a few hours ago, after we shared grilled cheese sandwiches and had a "story meeting" for the upcoming Monday paper.

"We have always marked time with babies. It is a way of measuring accomplishments," he said to me.

I was immediately frightened by his use of the plural. Was the "we" he was talking about old money Yankees. He certainly wasn't speaking for his young girlfriend, Sevina. You certainly don't mark time with babies when you are 22.

"Do you want to see my house," Elise asks me.

"Sometime," I say looking at her wedding ring.

"Good answer," she tells me, launching into what sounds to be a well-rehearsed summation of her personal life.

Her story is that she has been married and living on St. Simon for three years. Her husband, who she names only by that possessive phrase, spends a week at a time on St. Croix where he is the croupier at the new casino.

"It was a career opportunity that we decided he couldn't pass up, especially while we are building a house," Elise said, as if it was now obvious what was going to happen next.

I wondered quickly if I had anything to do the next day as we got into her Jeep and pulled out of the driveway. Estate Carolina was a 25 minute drive so Elise lit a cigarette and gave me an opener for the wine.

"Hold on," she said, pulling over to the side of the road and putting out her cigarette only a few hundred yards into the journey.

"I'm not going to take you all the way out to my house if you aren't a good kisser."

Feeling the pressure of this audition I struggled to brush her smoky lips with the most gentle five Heineken kiss I could muster. She met my lips seeming to plead for my tongue, which I gave her the littlest taste of.

And she bit it, the bitch, breaking the kiss and slamming the car into first gear in the same motion.

When we arrived in Estate Carolina the power was out and we had to drink wine and talk about writing.

"I'll let you make love to me," she said, "but I want to get to know you."

I got the tour of the new construction. A nearly full lopsided moon cradled the Milky Way and desire took a back seat to eternity. I quietly pissed in a delicate arc off the railing into the jungle below and thought about Jenny's beautiful face. I decided that was the vision I would see when I closed my eyes.

Upstairs Elise was lighting candles and looking for batteries to play an Enya tape.

When she came downstairs I peeled down her dress and sucked gently at her nipples until she turned around and ground herself into my hard on.

"I want you to tie me up," she said and I agreed.

She awoke at dawn and rustled me because she had to go to the health club and then to work. Her guilt led her out to the verandah to find the wine from the night before and search for any solace a big slug would offer.

She showered and donned an equally absurd flowered print dress and hustled me into her jeep. She grabbed a book by a German writer I had never heard of and gave it to me, asking me to keep my distance.

"I do you like your cock, though," she said pulling out and racing towards Roach Harbor. I didn't speak, my head hurt. Hints of pink and blue were in the sky from the rising sun. The landscape was beginning to become clear as we raced up and down the mountains. As we approached Botnay Bay there was a jet-black stream of smoke darting up into the morning sky. Elise barely slowed as we zipped past the two new blue dumpsters, fully engaged in fire, flames licking at the arriving dawn.

The fire trucks passed us as we descended Ski Slope hill and started into Roach Harbor. As we got near the *The Melee* and the Green Tree Inn where we met, Elise veered off the road, nearly into a ditch and stopped the Jeep, much like she had done on the way out of town.

This time she said, "I'm married, I can't drive through town with you in the car at this hour."

I rubbed my sleepy eyes and kissed her goodbye.

Stepping from the Jeep I felt her lips still on my cheek and my mind began to spin. Walking home I thought of another thing the Publisher told when he was talking about marking time with sex and babies.

"St. Simon," he said. "is a great place to reinvent yourself."

chapter 10

Four – Twenty

So I'm walking up the hill to *The Melee* with my head still throbbing, sort of wondering what happened to me last night and hoping there isn't a big line at the bakery.

Well, there is a big line, most people on St. Simon get up early. And of course I see Jenny in line for coffee, because sometimes St. Simon is like a small college campus and you can't avoid anyone. And Jenny is with Hillary, which threatens any anonymity I might have wrongfully thought was mine.

They have a funny roll and stumble look to them like they have been up all night and I'm immediately perplexed. Hillary is old school St. Simon, I know her parents lived here and some of her aunts and uncles. If I made a family tree of the old St. Simon white people she would be able to crawl out and hang on numerous branches.

Now she knows Jenny. Yikes.

Jenny may be a cop, she may be a future girlfriend, she may be pissed at me for not calling her, but right now it looks like she is a little drunk.

Then it dawns on me from a spare part of my head that I forgot existed. It is Friday, April 20. What this means, and if you know Hillary this somehow makes sense, is that it is 4-20. And 4:20 is the international getting stoned time. Each day, for all these young

Phish fans and white dreadlocked trustafarians who have spread out all over the world, 4:20, a.m. or p.m., is the time they light up. I was warned Hillary would be waking everybody up at 3:50 a.m. on April 20 for a group smoke-out. For days now she had been going on about gathering on the beach in Roach Harbor at 4:20 a.m. on April 20.

"We came looking for you," the red-eyed Hillary tells me. "You are in trouble Mr. Hunger."

Jenny didn't really seem to be capable of speech at this early morning juncture so, thankfully we didn't have to talk. I knew I must smell of Elise or at least her horrible cigarettes.

"I knew you were coming so I went camping," I told Hillary. "Happy 4-20 ladies!"

I caught Jenny's sunflower eyes with this holiday greeting and was stuck. The soft brown tones made me feel safe in a way I knew I shouldn't.

"Somebody must be awfully disappointed with your boss," Jenny said to me.

I looked at her quizzically and just said "yup," because somebody was always disappointed with Caleb, and the list of who might be upset on this particular spring day was too much for my small head.

"Have you seen his car," Jenny said.

"Oh yeah," I said, figuring somebody had slashed Caleb's tires. Usually when Caleb was being unreasonable somebody would give a local kid a $10 bill to slash the Publisher's tires and keep him close to home for a while.

"Caleb's grounded again, huh?" I offered.

"I expect to see you on the beach this afternoon," Hillary interrupted, breaking the spell of Jenny's soft eyes.

"I don't know," I said.

"Jenny and I will meet you at your house and if you aren't there you will really be in trouble," Hillary told me.

I wondered how much trouble. Could this Ivy League girl really want to hang out with the likes of Hillary and me in an endless 4:20 Caribbean sunshine life?

I caught myself frozen in my brain. I was wondering whether Hillary knew what she was doing when in fact, I concluded, I was the one who was pushing the envelope of secrecy, good taste and reality a little too far.

I paid for my coffee and sticky bun and told the girls I would see them at my house, later on.

Down Island

chapter 11

Friday's News Stories

As soon as I got my bearings on Friday morning I spit out three news stories like they were vomit.

Not so curiously I felt like I caused them all. I also felt physically sick to my stomach from all that drinking I did with Elise. Putting any and all thoughts of conflict of interest and morality aside I just sat down with my sticky bun and started typing. I couldn't help looking up at a poem I had taped to my computer at the newspaper. It was mailed to the newspaper by a friend and frequent contributor, but it never made it by the Publisher's watchful eye and into print. Still I thought it summed up *The Melee* pretty well so I saved it.

The Island Melee
by Mike Ellis

The joke is big
at the island newspaper
and it expands in hilarity
and absurdity
banner headlines
streaming above the fold

It gets funnier

throughout the season
every story adding to the joke
each next issue
even more fantastic
every copy selling

In the early summer
when the last souvenirs
are sold
the breezes die down
and the air becomes still
violently, the joke implodes

We drag its dead weight
out to the beach
or better yet, send it off
to re-hab
the once grand joke
now old and sad.

But it washes up in October
familiar and swelling,
with new shoes on
resilient legs, the joke
is splashed on the front page
ripe for the telling.

I was really hoping to just accurately describe what I saw without falling prey to the subtleties implied in the poem. But the surrounding facts which people really want to know about most of the news stories in *The Melee* simply had to be implied by innuendo. The stories were too complex so I was forced to use a sort of "calypso style" for lack of a better phrase, to explain the effect of ongoing events.

You see, the idea at *The Melee* has always been to avoid direct accusations while raising questions and concerns about our public safety and infrastructure, and with some dramatic editing from Caleb, subtly point a few fingers at any corruption that might be involved.

For the first story all I had to do was look out the window across the street at the carcass of the company vehicle. The other stories seemed like dreams that occurred to me during a nap in the hot sun. Vivid, hot and scary.

Fire Guts Melee Vehicle in Roach Harbor

By Don Hunger
Melee Staff

The charred and melted body of the burned-out Chevy Blazer gleamed in the morning light on April 20.

An infant's change of clothes with its sleeves and pant legs singed off lends a macabre air to the stark scene.

The short-lived fire had been so intense that only the metal hardware left was from an infant car seat that had been in the middle of the back seat.

The inside of the four-door vehicle, once a Chevy Blazer, is now a stark metal shell. Everything plastic in the vehicle formed a layer of ash around a handful of unidentifiable charred and melted objects on the floor of the passenger side of the truck.

Melted chunks of window glass sparkle in the black soot.

The fabric and foam of all but a small corner of the bench back seat are gone. The front bucket seats are spindly frames of metal tubing and springs.

The dashboard is a frozen mass of melted plastic suspended on the charred wires of radios and instruments.

The bright colors of family pictures shine in the charred papers of the melted glove box. The remains of the hard plastic door handles and vehicle insignia are scattered on the ground.

The back tailgate is a crumbling pile of charred fiberglass. The left rear tire and spare are both partially incinerated.

The gas cap is a hardened glob of plastic hanging from the lip of the fill pipe, the gas tank miraculously unexploded.

Someone had apparently used the "Jaws of Life" to crack open the hood of the vehicle - only to find the fire had not spread from the interior of the car to the engine compartment.

The Thursday, April 19, incident was recorded by the Roach Harbor Police Department at 11:22 p.m. as a "reported car fire."

The fire scene was relatively undisturbed when fire officials finally inspected the scene approximately 10 hours later.

Mysterious Fire
solves St. Simon Trash woes

By Don Hunger
Melee Staff

Dancing flames looked liked they wanted to kiss the dawn sky Friday morning as a dumpster conflagration solved a nagging trash collection problem.

Fire department officials responded shortly after the break of day to the dumpsters shared by residents of Botnay Bay and Great Roach Harbor to find flames shooting nearly 15 feet into the air from two new giant blue dumpsters recently purchased with private neighborhood funds.

Dark smoke and smells of burning household trash blanketed the neighborhood bays suffocating the normal smells of brewing coffee, sizzling bacon and blooming frangipani.

Only days earlier in the office of *The Melee* Mayor Eustis Smith lamented the troubling trash situation, which rendered island garbage trucks bent and broken by the new dumpsters, which, it turned out, were too heavy for the Department of Public Works garbage trucks to lift up and unload.

"I don't know what the hell we are going to do," the Mayor commented privately last week.

The fire, one of two mysterious blazes on St. Simon between the final hours of April 19 and sunrise the following day, offered a short term solution to the redolent trash overflow problem, an anonymous DPW worker observed.

"Trash gone now meh son," he noted.

The new bins, which were paid for by residents of the two affluent St. Simon neighborhoods arrived three weeks ago and were placed out for homeowners to dispose of household trash. The bins were already overflowing two weeks ago when Public Works officials learned that their garbage trucks were not equipped to empty them.

The answer to Smith's public prayers came at dawn Friday when the suspicious fire reduced the mountains of trash that had accumulated to ash which floated in clouds over the islands South Shore. The fire charred the new dumpsters, peeling back the paint and giving them the well-worn look of the former trash receptacles.

Smith was not available for comment on what might be done to solve the larger problem of the overweight dumpsters or for comment on whether there were any repercussions in store for any supposed arsonists involved in the blaze.

By noon on Friday, residents had already filled the emptied dumpsters to near half capacity with household trash that had, no doubt, been piling up in homes over the past week.

National Park Mooring Balls slashed in apparent random act of Vandalism

By Don Hunger
Melee Staff

"They looked like giant striped ping-pong balls floating towards St. Thomas," said one anonymous liveaboard boater who photographed the mysterious site for The Melee.

The "ping-pong balls" floating in the ocean were approximately half of the 200 new National Park mooring balls which had recently been installed thanks to local and Federal government funds. Officials confirmed Thursday that sometime in the pre-dawn hours of April 19, an unknown person or persons had severed the lines to the pleasure boat moorings. Nearly every mooring that wasn't being used that morning was slashed and allowed to simply drift away.

"This was no random act of vandalism," an irate Virgin Island National Park Superintendent Clive Duke told *The Melee*. "Somebody planned this out."

The mooring lines that were slashed were half-inch thick nylon line. The mooring balls were secured to three sand screws sunk into the ocean floor. The moorings arrived only six months earlier and were installed in the National Park waters. Local officials said they were concerned that the constant anchoring of vessels was wreaking havoc with the undersea life. The moorings had been hailed as a gift from the heavens by marine biologists.

Duke placed the cost of the vandalism at approximately $150,000. Residents who might find mooring balls may return them to National Park offices on St. Thomas or St. Simon, Duke said.

"I am ordering a full police investigation by the Coast Guard," said Duke who recently arrived on St. Simon from his former post at Grand Canyon National Park.

Down Island

chapter 12

Bomba

Having three juicy news stories in the can takes a load off my mind.

I realize it shouldn't be a stress situation, but I like *The Melee* to look nice and be interesting. It has my name on it.

And everyone reads it. Oh they say they don't, but they do. They will swear they don't read the paper and in the same sentence quote you a line from it.

Rolling years back, after a curious murder of a black man, the Publisher started linking some of the white expatriates in Fort Bay to the Klu Klux Klan. That didn't go over too well. People hated the Publisher so much he hired me to write the paper. There were some petitions and boycotts but the Publisher, much to his credit, wouldn't quit. He still won't budge. He may be a prick but he fancies himself a true old school news man. If he even remotely believes something is true, he will run with it.

I would like to move on, separate myself from his madness, especially on these days when the spotlight from the Coconut Telegraph seems brighter than the sun. Eustis Smith is a powerful man on St. Simon. He could easily have me burn up like the Publisher's car. The smugglers whose reservations I canceled a few nights before just may have uglier plans for me. They are certainly more dangerous. The lack of control you have over a situation in the Caribbean can be completely unsettling if you bother thinking about it.

I daydream of transcending the islands, taking the money I have buried in various holes in the ground and running for the safety of a suburb. Maybe work at a real newspaper again or try and be a writer.

But I wonder if I can go back after all these years. I know the Publisher can't. Everyone is too straight in America. Long periods in a lawless society have a funny way of changing a person. I couldn't imagine really taking orders, so to speak, from a boss. Or commuting? Goodness no.

I left work at *The Melee* refreshed from an afternoon nap on the company couch and joined some of the regulars on the beach in Roach Harbor for the 4-20, 4:20 p.m. celebration.

"What's up bro?"

I felt like Norm at a tropical Cheers.

Thankfully it was a quiet scene with glass pipes full of stinky weed being discretely passed around. Of course nobody had a watch so the exact 4:20 p.m. party celebration sort of lost that New Year's Eve countdown routine, which seemed fine by everyone.

"Close enough for St. Simon," said Hillary, who like a good Girl Scout made a sun dial in the sand with a forgotten sailboat batten. Eventually everyone was smiling and talking and the afternoon passed like so many others. Curiously Jenny didn't show up and I asked Hillary about it.

"I could tell you have a thing for her," she told me. "She's like you, I couldn't get her out of bed, even for afternoon 4:20."

Another weird day behind me I was making my way up the hill when I saw Judy in her golf cart.

"Happy 4-20!," I tell this sprightly ninety-something, who is clad in a Rasta style knit cap, possibly for the occasion.

I hop in next to her and her little dog for a ride up the hill and I'm immediately pulled into Judy's world and the events surrounding her small hilltop compound where I reside in a small one-room bungalow. The golf cart parked I find myself repositioning an ancient air conditioner and funneling its drip into a small grove of hibiscus plants.

Judy rewarded me with a slice of pizza from the bakery and I found my way into my favorite afternoon seat, high above Roach Harbor on the deck of my small bungalow.

An hour passed and I began to get lonely, lost in thoughts about escaping St. Simon and fearful for the trouble I had been leaving in my wake all week long.

Jenny was a blooming flower when she drove up in a borrowed Suzuki Jeep and beeped. She had two yellow kayaks on the roof and a big smile.

"Time for adventure," she explained, refusing a kiss.

"I'm ready for anything," I told her, backing it up with a smile. I grabbed a few things out of the fridge, locked the doors to my bungalow and we immediately set off.

We made quick time, skirting Roach Harbor, which was winding up for the weekend at this point.

All the traffic was going the other way as we sped towards the country. Contractors driving pick-up trucks with beds full of construction workers, all bound for Roach Harbor. Their smiles told us they had paychecks in their pockets. I knew shortly they would either be in line at one of the two ATM's on the island or jammed behind the bar in one of the new Spanish language watering holes that cater largely and happily to the influx of immigrant workers. Unlike the Chinese these workers from down island have no intention of leaving St. Simon for the mainland. They want to make some money and go back home.

I doubt mainstream America's news companies believe or care that this island could be the front lines of any international human smuggling ring. The façade is too mellow. My conjecture is that the stateside editors have been so busy behind their desks that they don't have time to know the rhythm or the trials of any other cultures. And the last thing they want is a new complicated story to worry about.

We parked the borrowed jeep near the Glucksberg Sugar Mill and walked the kayaks across the road to a small beach hidden in the mangroves. First we took a quick inventory. One bottle of Gatorade, some cookies, four bananas, $32, an Advantage telephone card and no identification.

Our mission was clear as the tropical ocean. We would paddle for West End, Tortola and hopefully make landfall within two hours. We would stow the kayaks not too long after sunset and watch the moon rise. Then it would be time to walk up and over Zion Hill and down toward Bomba's Shack in Apple Bay for his full moon beach party.

chapter 13

Full Moon Find

A big plate of fungi and fish and Jenny's brown eyes made me forget the trappings of reality that congested my brain all week. Before I had two cold greenies in me I was socializing like a tourist. The traditional full moon party at Bomba's beach shack has been written up in a number of glossy magazines over the years, and although somewhat cheapened by its newfound popularity, it is still usually a lot of fun.

"Are you flirting with these men?," Jenny asked me, as she led me to the beach for a dance away from the crowd.

Of course Hillary and some of her friends were on the beach. Goodness knows how they arrived or how they would get home.

"Can you believe it," Hillary yelled. "Full moon on 4-20, this is the Super Bowl."

We swayed with the music and felt the rhythm of the sea and sand and I remembered why I was in the West Indies. More beer and some handpicked mushrooms appeared as the moon climbed straight overhead. Back at Bomba's Shack the tourists were lining up for mushroom tea and rocking the beach bar. More revelers joined all the young St. Simon hippies on the beach and drum circles erupted. We danced and danced in the cooling sand and my cares seemed to blow away in the soft breezes of the Caribbean night.

I reached for Jenny's hand and watched the reflection of the moon cascade off the water and make a direct line for us. I felt like I belonged. We didn't have to speak.

Time seemed to vanish with everyone getting worn out but Jenny and me. The revelers slowly dissipated. Only Bomba's son was left at the bar as we prepared for our walk back up and over Zion Hill to the hidden yellow kayaks.

"Don Hunger, you and you lady are de King and de Queen of de ball, for true," Bomba Jr., said, offering us both a dark Tennant's Stout for the walk home.

We thanked him and Jenny took off her necklace, a lovely red fish carved from coral hanging from a leather strap. She put it around his neck.

"You are the Prince," she told our friend, and I knew then I was in love with her.

The moon led us to the kayaks and we kissed madly before wedging our tired bodies into the skinny hulls. The stars were just beginning to fade as we pushed off the sand and paddled out into the current.

Sir Francis Drake Channel always flows west towards St. Thomas where the moon was sinking into the still twinkling lights of Crown Mountain before us. Behind us the sun was beginning to rise on our backs. We didn't have to paddle in the tide but we did, which gave us that same feeling of quickness you get when you walk on one of those flat escalators in the airport.

Out of nowhere one cloud appeared in the sunrise and we were doused with a mini-monsoon. We laughed like wet rats still high from the party. When it cleared we saw a rainbow and then I knew I was still really high because I was paddling in and out of the bars of color, staring in wonderment at the scene and in awe of Jenny.

"We are part of the rainbow," she announced, finding words again after more than an hour of silence on the flat Caribbean Sea.

Just as she spoke I saw the dorsal fin break the water not five yards behind her. She saw the terror in my eyes and turned quickly but could not find a scream.

"Follow me," I said, paddling.

Great Thatch Cay, an uninhabited British rock just off St. Simon's North Shore and safety were in sight. I lost speech and I started to pee myself. But I continued paddling. The shark disappeared and then surfaced again just to my right. At that point I couldn't paddle anymore and Jenny saw this.

"Now you follow me," she said in a high-pitched squeal. Bravely she indicated the coordination necessary to paddle to shore and safety. I found my motor skills and we pushed it hard for the beach on Great Thatch. We heard the shark breaking the water and felt the unseen threat chasing us for nearly 100 yards. We paddled the boats right straight up on to the beach. Seated in the boats, we were both temporarily unable to begin prying ourselves out of the kayaks. Instead we concentrated on breathing. Eventually our eyes converged on what looked like two hay bales wrapped in white plastic garbage bags sitting idly on the edge of the surf and the coral sand in the bright morning sun. We got out of the kayaks and hugged. Then, as we began to investigate, it all suddenly dawned on me like a psychedelic sunrise.

Two bales of the cocaine from the night the reservations were canceled were sitting there on the deserted beach.

Down Island

Part 2
chapter 14

Jenny Speaks

*W*ell, yes, I am a cop.

And yes, it is obvious that I have crossed a few lines, let alone international borders and serious protocol barriers drawn much deeper than lines in the St. Simon sand. That is just how it stood.

When the FBI came to Vassar I was the perfect candidate. I was in the top of my class but I was still impressionable. I never took drugs in college. I rarely partied. I studied.

But I also yearned for adventure. I grew up in small town in southern New Hampshire and never really learned to socialize correctly. I never had money either.

So after a year at Quantico when the FBI decided they wanted to set me up with a jewelry business in St. Simon I accepted immediately. First I went home to Rollinsford, New Hampshire, moved back in with my folks and started taking a jewelry class at the University of Southern Maine in Portland.

"Have you lost your mind, Jen?" my mother once asked me abruptly in the street when she saw me clad in a hippie dress and a silly hemp necklace, chatting it up with kids from the current

high school class in front of a coffee shop in nearby Dover.

Of course my parents thought I was crazy. I couldn't tell them anything. I just went to jewelry school and tried to blend in with hippie kids my own age. It was weird.

My parents stopped asking questions when I showed them a stub from one of my paychecks. I gave my mother a few expense checks and she bought a new car. After that she had no problem telling her friends that her daughter Jen was taking jewelry classes and trying to "find" herself.

It was fun being a 23- year old girl again. I would go months without talking with any of my superiors. I started to talk and act like a person my age, or more accurately someone around 17.

Truthfully, my superiors were not really even that worried about the human smuggling trade that was funneling droves of Chinese through St. Simon. They just wanted to keep an eye on it. If I saw a suspicious Arab, and there were a few, I immediately had to file a full report.

Oh sure, one of my expressed goals was to try and infiltrate the drug smuggling pipeline and see who was heading up the operations in St. Maarten and in the Virgin Islands. But the FBI isn't that interested in boat pirates on the U.S., French or British islands. This perplexed me, but they seemed to have little, if any, concern for the drug traffic that went through the islands. It was like they already had a handle on it, like it was pre-ordained. Most locals suggested the local cops had their own deal with the FBI.

For months my only contribution to the FBI was to mail copies of The Virgin Island Daily News stories about the aliens, along with any other information on the Chinese I could gather, to another agent in Florida who would put them in another envelope and mail them to Washington D.C.

This was my introduction to Don Hunger and Caleb. They would write all kinds of crazy stuff about the aliens. They refused to take it too seriously but at the same time they were spot on. Their main concern was that the aliens were not getting enough to eat while they were in lock-up. Before the local authorities squashed it, they had restaurants bringing gourmet leftovers to the dripping wet

Chinese in their improvised holding pens at the police station.

They also stood up for their dignity. For months they would editorialize about the fact that the aliens were handcuffed on the ferry boat ride to federal court in St. Thomas while other more dangerous criminals were not "cuffed" on the boat, a right afforded to native Virgin Island criminals who seem to have an innate fear of the water.

The policy changed but it changed back as soon as The Melee pointed out that they had elicited a change in the name of human rights.

For a while Don and Caleb were trying to find sponsors for the aliens and open an authentic Chinese restaurant. I had never seen irreverence like this in the news and I was hooked. In a way I felt like I was part of a big inside joke. I would not forward The Melee stories to the FBI for fear they would start a file on these far out writers. Eventually I would figure out that the FBI probably already had a file on Don and Caleb in Washington, probably bigger than anything I could ever put together.

And that is how my defection into the freedom of private citizenship started. I'm not a jeweler, but I was playing one in Roach Harbor. And I'm not a hippie. And I didn't even try to act like one. But I made friends, lots of friends, by just being myself.

Finally I felt like I belonged. The minute I felt comfortable with my St. Simon community, the FBI lost all of its allure. It would have been a different story, maybe, if I was actually trying to help the aliens.

Oh sure, it was a motley crew I belonged to on St. Simon, but I felt like I belonged. I would walk into Roach Harbor some mornings as the bar flies were rowing out to their floating hotels in the harbor with stolen batteries to charge their portable air conditioners and we would exchange the pleasantries of commuters. Minutes later I would greet rich snowbirds who would come in and ask me to design jewelry for them. I surmised that it was the island life that made everyone seem equal. I was never really trying to make money so I treated everyone right.

After I found Eustis Smith's wife's wallet in the street and returned *it personally to their house up in Contant, they never failed to go out of their way to be nice to me. I dated surfers, minor league pirates and sailors who lived from whatever the wind blew their way. I dated a street poet named Stuart for a while. He would rant and rave in the bars until people would pay him to go away. Then he would steal flowers from the cemetery and show up at my door with some treasure he found in the street.*

It was romantic and beautiful. Just like St. Simon.

But it was sad too. Every morning a gaunt streetwalker named Socrates would come by, after wandering the streets all night in a narcotic stupor, drinking half empty leftover beers and laughing madly. For nearly a year he asked me for money. After two years he began to talk to me. Socrates had been wandering the streets of Roach Harbor, barefoot and drunk for as long as anyone could remember. Most people didn't even know he could talk. I felt like his family.

I already knew Don when he walked out to Superman's beach one morning and introduced himself by just that common first name. The thing about him and Caleb that immediately perplexed me was the way they took giant stock in St. Simonians. Something could have happened, say a governmental issue or a debate over where the Post Office should go, and Don and Caleb would immediately defer to the old timers. They were far more interested in what the guy on the street thought than any spin Eustis Smith or the governor wanted to put on something. (Later, of course I realized that the officials simply wouldn't talk to them anymore).

Still the whole island of St. Simon seemed to subscribe to a sort of sliding scale of expertise based solely on who had been on St. Simon longer. The natives opinions came first, then the "born here" people like Superman and then the old timers like Judy and this guy who looks like Tiny Tim who owns the Lobster Trap restaurant and the car rental.

The theory that Don and Caleb seemed to support was that anyone who hadn't found St. Simon and dug in by the late 1980's probably had nothing worthwhile to say.

It infuriated the new white people and when I slowly realized that the joke was on them I laughed even louder.

Of course I played dumb when I met Don. And, with a remarkably straight face, so did he. I remember him asking me if I had ever seen The Melee. *Well I had been on St. Simon for two years by the time I started hanging out with this quirky guy, so of course I had seen* The Melee. *It was in your face every Monday whether you wanted to see it or not.*

And of course I had seen him, countless times, running around town with bare feet and a beer or maybe a disposable camera in his hand. He struck me immediately as someone without a care in the world. I thought he might be, you know, touched, at first, because he smiled so much.

And I know for a fact he had seen me. I don't mean to flatter myself but even the plainest of young women are noticed by all the male population of St. Simon the minute they arrive on island. All the men on St. Simon are lecherous in a sort of predatory but slightly charming way.

But, that first morning, we both pretended we had never seen each other before.

I guess it was just the dance we had to do.

Down Island

chapter 15

cool change

I had not crossed this line before.

It was a big stretch. You just don't accidentally trip over lines with the Federal Bureau of Investigations. But you do fall.

All Special Agent Jenny Hayes really had to do was monitor this current Chinese alien invasion into the U.S. Virgin Islands and, of course, keep my eyes open. Cavorting with beach bums and shady no-accounts was not forbidden, in fact it was even encouraged for background purposes.

But as I became integrated into St. Simon society I started hiding things. One of my girlfriends got hooked on crack cocaine. I wrestled with her for a few months, watched her begin to whore herself, then I just called her mother back in St. Louis and bought her a plane ticket. I even expensed it.

I had gotten flip too. I had taken to wearing a t-shirt that said FBI on it in big letters and "female body inspector" below it. Lesbian tourists would hit on me at the shop and at the Tiki Bar next door where I spent too much time. It was like I was having my first teenage rebellion now at age 25.

I would close the shop for two days in the middle of season and go to the beach or just stay home and smoke pot and watch Bonanza re-runs on cable, stuff the other girls did at Vassar without me. The freedom was intoxicating. I think I had too much too fast. I was beginning to see things in a completely different light. I was losing my hold. All that brainwashing the FBI had provided for me was starting to slip away, the same way my cares would be lost in the breeze when I got in a convertible jeep and cruised through the countryside.

My supervisors had warned me about going native, but all along I reassured them in my reports.

But the FBI has big eyes and it was like they knew all along I was weak. On April 19 they contacted me through Eustis Smith's office at the Battery. I had never seen the Mayor more perplexed than when he had to come to my jewelry store to deliver a packet from the federal government. On this beautiful spring day on this tucked away outpost of an island I was reassigned to work in Washington D.C.

I was in shock. No more beach parties, no more Rastamen, no more drugs, NO MORE DAYS AT THE BEACH. I was in shock. I closed the shop and went to the Beach Bar and stared into the harbor. I couldn't stop thinking about the beauty. I wondered if it was fake.

I was still drunk and stoned when Hillary came up to get me shortly before 4 a.m. the next morning for the 4-20 celebration. My traveling orders were spread out on the table. I lay awake in bed, wondering if the FBI knew what 4:20 meant.

I was having nightmares of uptight Georgetown dinner parties, tight leather shoes and pantsuits. I was tossing and turning and twisting up my sheets when I heard Hillary's Boston accent and smokers hack in driveway.

I knew then I had seen too much. I knew that I somehow belonged with the crazy people in this fragile and beautiful place. I still hadn't crossed the line, but I wanted to.

That's when Hillary walked into my house and saw the FBI package on my kitchen table.

"Don't tell me you are doing your freaking income tax on 4-20, sister, come on, get your Chucks on, we're going to the beach."

Why not, I thought. Why not live like the world might end tomorrow. Why not live like the FBI wasn't running the show. I wasn't doing anything that countless other 25- year old women who didn't want to get trapped in a suburb weren't doing.

I partied with Hillary all morning and refused to open the shop or call the FBI in favor of a long afternoon nap. When I awoke I read my traveling orders again and realized that I would be passing up a lot of money and opportunity if I didn't go to Washington D.C.

But when you start kayaking to other countries to eat mushrooms and dance on the beach all night with the most irreverent members of the Fourth Estate you are, in FBI lingo, pushing the envelope. But I didn't feel like I completely crossed the line. Even when I asked the shady boy in question to make love to me under the full moon, beneath the panoply of stars and within a liberating haze of magic mushrooms on a remote beach in the British Virgin Islands, I didn't feel out of line. I hardly felt like I was an outlaw.

But the minute you start hauling bales of cocaine up into the jungle of the National Park to bury them for future sale THEN things have changed. Fortunately for me, that is what I was looking for. Something new.

Down Island

chapter 16

Down Island

I t was simple, just like things like this never are.

We beached the kayaks on Johnson's Bay and hiked the heavy bales of hooch up a hill and into the National Park. It was still early in the morning, nobody saw us. We covered the bales with leaves and trees and looped Catch-n-Keep around them and split as fast as we could. We were still really too flustered to have a conversation.

Scratched and bleeding from the bush we hiked back to the kayaks and paddled to Glucksberg to get Jenny's borrowed car. We still hadn't really spoken. Finally, after securing the boats on the roof and getting on the road home, Jenny took her eyes from her hands, which white knuckled the wheel on the deserted country road. She turned to me dead pan and said, "Act nonchalant when we get to town."

It took and we laughed hard together. We became one scared voice.

I had my secrets and I felt hers. But this was new and it was our voice. It startled us both.

So now its come to this for me, I thought during the silent ride back to my bungalow; I've got two hay bales of cocaine in the jungle, my life savings is buried in the ground and I've got a new girlfriend/business partner that I don't know from Adam.

I had to quit my job at the newspaper, sell the drugs and sort of casually disappear with my money before any number of gruesome scenarios unfolded and crushed me.

And I guess I had to figure out how to do this pronto.

Maybe I knew I had to go the minute I called the dinner reservations off. Maybe this was a good excuse to go in style. Maybe not. My guess was that I should have left this particular beach party a long time ago.

My ticket to freedom was already buried in the ground on St. Simon. It was in the form of stacks of unmarked fifty and hundred dollar bills from the drug running business. There was probably $80,000 in my underground account. Plenty to get me set up most any place besides New York or San Francisco and I wasn't about to go to a city anyway. I already had more than I needed. I really had it all, but I should have realized that before I complicated the dinner reservation drop-off the previous Sunday night.

Still I felt I had enough money to get out with a clean nose and a nice profit, and it was time to go. I had kept the cover of working as a newspaper reporter for long enough that it felt like a career. But that was before we found the dope, practically on our doorstep. Now, in some weird way, I resented these bales of cocaine. They had become baggage for Christ's sake, but it was my fault we found them.

I still really had to wonder if Jenny was a cop. Of course if she was, I was totally fried because the minute she put that fish necklace of hers around Bomba's son's neck I fell completely in love with her. Everything changed in my head. She sealed the deal when she lifted the bales of cocaine on her back and hoofed up into the bush with me.

So now its come to this for me, I thought as I drove to newspaper man Don Hunger's bungalow as he dozed off in the passenger seat.

I have barely turned 25 and I am now looking at becoming an international outlaw all so I can spend time with some dumb boy who can barely put out a weekly newspaper without getting himself killed. But I did feel alive.

I could go to Washington D.C. and live the most boring life in the world or I could get on this ride, which doesn't seem like it ever slows down. I don't think my parents would even recognize me. My hair has grown out, I have bags under my eyes from being up all night, cuts and scratches all over my arms from hauling drugs through the jungle and blisters on my hands from paddling away from sharks.

I saw it all so clear, too, for just a brief instant, in that rainbow. I saw myself as a free woman. A woman who didn't have to file a report to the FBI or to her parents. A woman in harmony with nature, able to paddle against the current, dry her eyes in the wind and wrap herself in the puffy clouds and sleep the sleep of a warrior.

Then the shark showed up.

I guessed it was time to grow up. I had to come clean with the FBI. Tell them everything I learned about the aliens and suggest to them I was better suited to be a child of the earth, not a snoop for the government.

I could make jewelry anywhere. That was starting to really work. I could grow things like my grandfather did in the fields of Dover, Rochester and Rollinsford New Hampshire. I could stay with this boy or I could dust him if he wasn't up to my challenge. I was on my own for the first time in that rainbow. I didn't have the FBI, I didn't have my parents, I didn't have any friends and I didn't mind.

At my bungalow I keep a case of Heineken on hand in case I have to do any real thinking. I put half of it in the freezer the minute we got home from stashing the drugs. It was still early, about 11 a.m. and we hadn't been to sleep for well over a day. We were too hungry and bewildered to immediately sit down and weigh our options. We were still too wired from the drugs and the recent events to sleep.

I defrosted Bratwurst and made a cheese omelet with extra-firm tofu and spinach. Jenny began toasting bread and didn't stop. Outside the yellow Dancing Lady orchids and light blue petreas decorated the bungalow. The March drought was over and red and purple bougainvillea bloomed everywhere. The air was thick with jasmine. It was a tropical heaven. We went back inside anyway and finished eating, oblivious to the natural wonder.

We talked, finally, and I wondered privately who Jenny was.

She took out a pad and paper and started to rattle off our options.

I played a Hank Williams Greatest Hits C.D. through the tinny portable speakers that hook up to my Sony disc player.

Jenny talked about going to New Hampshire.

We both drank cold greenies.

Jenny cried. I wanted to cry too, but I was too scared.

We tried to make love but knew it was stupid at that scared and drunken juncture.

We remembered we were friends.

"Are you a cop?" I asked her straight out.

"Yes I am, but I won't bust you," she said without any hesitation. The remark caught me off guard and made the whole thing a little more mysterious.

We drank some beer and things got fuzzy. We slept for a while. Then, as if a day disappeared in a vacuum, the morning sun shook us at dawn. We had complicated our lives so much just 24 very strange hours earlier. I think it was Sunday morning.

I could inspect my entire combination kitchen, bedroom and living room home from my bed. My one room home was littered with beer bottles, kayak paraphernalia and empty plates of half eaten eggs and sausage. There was more beer frozen and ruined in the freezer. I felt sick but anxious. I realized I was late to put out *The Melee.*

On the table there were lists everywhere. All the options were crossed out except for one which must have battled it out in the finals with going to New Hampshire, or Bali for my best

recollection..
It read;
"Sail Down Island, ASAP."

Down Island

chapter 17

Liquid Bath

We split up, dividing the business at hand.

My job was to turn our jungle stash into cash.

Jenny was going to get us a low profile passage to someplace pretty and pretty far off the map. She went to see her people and I went to see mine.

In my head I scoured Roach Harbor, looking for someone with enough money to be interested in the cocaine and the lack of sense to get into the business. This was touchy. I had to sell the cache to someone who wasn't involved with any of the current drug dealers, people whom I didn't know. It couldn't be anyone who actually owned these expensive floating bales that I failed to pick up a week ago and discovered a few days later, either. So this person had to be an outlaw and they had to be rich or desperate. They also had to be smart enough to the see the deal through and make a profit of their own on the cocaine.

Or, I thought hopefully, just say a greedy drug addict with some happy cash would do fine.

Oh, and it had to be cash, because I was leaving town, but I couldn't tell anyone that. I was freaked out.

Jenny was in the bathroom.

I left her and the dirty bungalow to walk into Roach Harbor to find my future. The church bells chimed at Our Lady of Perpetual Reason.

Like it happens so often on St. Simon, the answer nearly ran me over as I walked down the driveway from my bungalow to go into town. It was Judy, in her golf cart. She had just been to church and then stopped at the Peace Pipe Market. Her golf cart was stacked full of cases of Heineken.

"Judy?" I said.

"I've got some Russians staying at the museum and they drink beer like water," this spunky woman explained.

"At least let them carry the beer home," I told Judy.

Judy arrived on St. Simon in the fifties, before cars. She taught school and threw wild parties with her Russian husband. Now well into her nineties, this wonderful widow has opened a museum to her memories. For many of the natives, and for me, Mrs. Sergenov will always be the very symbol of the school teacher. She was also my landlord and benefactor.

"I've got something to talk with you about, Judy."

"Don't tell me you don't have the rent. I know how hard you work. I will get it from Caleb myself," Judy said.

I got in the golf cart and we rode up to her hilltop museum. I unloaded the cases of beer while Judy, in a sort of hunched over frenzy, began preparing breakfast.

I spilled my guts. Judy, I knew, was one of the handful of old St. Simonians I could really trust. I told her about my semi-annual drug run. I knew she knew Carlos, my uncle and my father. All the old time white people, of which Judy was one of the first, knew Carlos. Judy also knew some of the natives who filled out this quiet drug cartel. Judy, in fact, knew more than I ever would have thought about this smuggling business that put more than a few kids, including myself, through college.

I told her everything. I needed to release it. I told her about Jenny. I told her about the money in the jungle. I told her about finding the bales and I told her I needed to get off the island.

She barely batted an eye as she disappeared for a few seconds into the inner-sanctums of her museum.

"This ring belonged to the President of Zanzibar," she told me when she returned with a tiny box in her hand.

In the box there was an enormous diamond. It was the kind of stone that seemed too big to be real.

I knew where she got it too. A woman named Lily came to the museum annually and lectured on Black history and Russian history. She had been married to the President of Zanzibar in 1962, before he was assassinated and his wealthy island seized by the Tanzanian government.

"I know you want to get married," Judy said to me. "But don't give this ring to Jenny. Turn it into some land. That's what's you need. Just a little land and you two can make a new life."

Judy, it turns out, struck up a friendship with Jenny not long after the young woman arrived. They were both Vassar alumnae.

"Thanks, Judy," I managed.

I didn't want to ask how much it was worth.

"I have no idea," Judy said, reading my mind. "Let me know when you find out. All I know is that you are better off with that than all those drugs and that dirty money."

"I love you, Judy," I told her, and we left it at that.

My situation was now so confusing I felt comfortable going to go see the stoned Publisher, no matter how angry he was at me for missing work.

I was accumulating wealth at a rapid pace and I really wondered what would happen to me. The Publisher had persuaded someone else to buy him the *New York Sunday Times* and it was littered around the office when I arrived. The paper was nearly done. Caleb handed me a picture of two National Park lifeguards inspecting some bales of cocaine that had washed up on Sugar Bay on Saturday.

"How do you like this headline," the Publisher asked me, showing off a prototype of the front page which read **PARADISE LOST?**

We got down to business quick. Caleb knew something big was afoot.

I suggested to the Publisher that he could have the cocaine I found at a fraction of its worth and he would eventually make enough money to finance a real home for him, his son and his sweet Israeli bride-to- be.

He jumped on the idea. Which made me nervous. He was hardly suspicious that I had two 40-pound bales of cocaine in the jungle. He called his mother for some money.

In the meantime I went back to the bungalow, fingered the many faceted marquise diamond, which was set squarely on a huge gold ring.

Could this really belong to me?

I looked around and something was different. The dishes were clean and the bed was made. Jenny had to be a cop.

I had to get rid of the drugs and go. I wondered if Jenny would come up with anything. I hoped that with the blessings from Judy at least I could actually find a new life. But what about this young woman who I was trying so hard not to be in love with?

I scoured the St. Simon telephone book looking for somebody with the right combination of money and shadiness to become the islands next big time cocaine dealer. I came up with about 25 names from the phone book. All candidates who might be able to raise about $100,000 in cash and were savvy enough (maybe) to make a huge profit for their trouble.

I wrote the names down and was overwhelmed with the prospect of trying to sell any of them all of this cocaine. Just then the Publisher knocked on my door and popped his head in the unlocked door.

"Deal me in," Caleb said.

He had his young son in one arm and a plastic bag with $18,000 in cash in the other. It was a fraction of what the uncut drugs were worth. I pretended to think it over for a brief second and said, "Yes."

I put the money in a blue duffel bag and hid it under the floorboards of my house. We got in Caleb's rented jeep and sped off to *The Melee*.

"Wait in the car," he said, leaving me parked nearly in the middle of the main street. Cars inched by on the right, the drivers shooting me looks, as I sat helpless in the passenger seat. Caleb appeared with two shovels, two machetes and two joints and spoke to me before getting in the jeep which sat running in the street.

"Don't worry, I gave the paper to the Conqueror," the Publisher said.

"You are still worried about *The Melee*?" he asked after a brief silence.

"I gotta go," I told him.

He jumped in the rental jeep and peeled out, just as Eustis Smith was trying to pull out of the road adjacent to *The Melee* offices. Completely cut off, the Mayor hit his brakes and jerked violently forward inside his Land Cruiser. Dressed in his Sunday church suit, the Mayor quickly recovered and shot us a cold silent stare that gave us both a silencing chill.

I was out of sweat, just running on adrenaline fumes as we hiked up into the bush. Caleb became drenched in sweat and I took his shovel from him. When we finally made it to the stash, Caleb was beside himself with the prospect of making some truly big money, for once. And unlike me, he would probably get off on the risk and excitement of it all.

He asked me who he should talk to about getting in on "the drop off" after these bales were sold.

I pretended like he was crazy and he didn't push it. We reburied the drugs in a better spot and I told him I was gone. He took it well, especially since I was the only one who knew where the bales were now buried and the only one he let help him with his newspaper.

At home later I treated my blisters in the sink. When my hands were clean I lifted the floorboards again and moved the money to a spot in the ceiling. The diamond was still zipped into my back pocket. My back was sore from digging in the hard Caribbean dirt. Caleb was little help in the jungle. But we had found him a secure hiding place and he put enough drugs in the wheel well of his rented jeep for him to self-medicate his family and begin a lucrative cash and carry business.

When Jenny arrived I had a lot to tell her. I completed my

mission, I had a diamond worth as much, if not more than the cocaine. And I was still in love.

Likewise, Jenny had found us a ride down island, but I wouldn't learn the details of that trip until much later on that sultry evening of languid celebration.

chapter 18

Suspicious Minds

*T*he minute we split up I became suspicious.

Everything I learned in the FBI told me not to trust Don Hunger. It was like he existed under an invisible umbrella of secrecy that I had never seen before.

I mean I watched him this morning when he left the bungalow. He saw his landlord Judy, who is in her nineties, and they sort of just smiled at each other like they were both in on this grand conspiracy. Thick as thieves. I immediately questioned the connection I felt with St. Simon because I wasn't here as long everybody else. I felt like it was a big charade being put on by a tight troupe of actors for my benefit.

My job today was to find us a quiet, unassuming way down island, or anyplace remote and wonderful, while Don would try to turn the cocaine into tons of cash to finance the trip. He volunteered for his half of the mission like it was doing the breakfast dishes. I resented him for taking the lead.

I, in fact, did the breakfast dishes in his one room bungalow, and let my mind race while I watched him out the window with his landlady.

What was this guy doing. How did he know EVERYBODY. Didn't

he grow up in the suburbs like everybody else I had ever really known.

And now, all of a sudden, I'm like attached to him in some inordinate way. I thought and thought but there wasn't anybody on St. Simon I could come up with who didn't know him first and better. I got scared and cried. I finished the dishes and made the bed and cried some more.

Then I went to Hillary for help. She was at the deli-counter at the Tropicale Superette and she looked worse than me.

"What it is, sister sunshine eyes," Hillary asked, mocking the circles under my eyes..

"It's complicated," I told her, "Do you know anyone going Down Island?"

Hillary looked at me like I was a math problem for a while.

"Karl is going to Antigua, do you know Karl?"

I didn't know Karl, but like all St. Simonians do, Hillary assures me that I did know him. When I insisted I didn't she describes him as a middle aged Danish man and asked again if I'm sure "I haven't met him, yet," like it was just a matter of time before our paths crossed.

"He was just in here ordering steaks for his trip," Hillary explained, as if that would have been a big help to me. Whatever the case it was a good lead, and I tumbled forward to Lands End Real Estate office to find Karl on the rooftop deck of the island's largest three story building.

A fu-manchu with an extended soul-patch decorating his face, I found Karl resting his hands and his gin and tonic on the porch railing. He was shirtless and squinting into the early afternoon sun, surveying the small town from above. I surmised that he was scanning the valley for potential home sites and the cash they might provide him. I met his eyes and watched them switch to thinking thoughts that were anything but invisible..

"Hey honey," he said, lighting a cigarette and clearly wondering if we had a drunken conversation he didn't remember.

Karl is a short, fat Dane. I'm sure he has seen me at the jewelry store, but to date he hadn't bothered to introduce himself because he is older than my father. I politely assure him we haven't met and in my best covert way tell him my friend and I want to go down to race week in Antigua and want to know if he needs a crew.

"You're with the kid from **The Melee***?" Karl asks me, his smile really starting to scare me.*

I nod, very uneasy with my new description, the Coconut Telegraph and the direction my life is going.

Down Island

chapter 19

Dan's Dogs

I blew out my flip flop
Stepped on a pop-top
Cut my foot and had to head on back home."

I found myself unconsciously singing along with Jimmy Buffet on the radio, possibly thinking it would help me go faster. Maybe I am just brainwashed by the marketing of paradise. Whatever the case I was humming along, unfazed by the bad drivers on their way to Sugar Bay in little tin can rental jeeps. I look just like them in the Suzuki I've borrowed from the Publisher to run errands, in fact we are all probably singing along with Jimmy.

I've heard that familiar Buffet song from radios on beaches and boats in the Virgin Islands for decades now but this time that one verse stops me in my tracks. I wonder desperately if Jenny even knows what a pop-top is. If she was my age she would have certainly made a necklace from dangerous aluminum tabs that used to seal countless millions of cans. But Jenny was not even born yet in the late seventies. She might have been born by 1980, but I'm not sure. She might not have the slightest idea what Jimmy Buffet is talking about when he says pop-top. They might have been phased out by the time she arrived on the scene. I made a mental note to ask her as I snapped off the radio.

Traversing the precipitous hills and random hairpin turns on my way to the old Gremlitz house, I consider stopping for a swim at Superman's Beach but do not. Minutes later the same thought runs through my head again at Sugar Bay but I convince myself I have important business to take care of.

I arrive at the old Gremlitz place, but I'll be darned if I'm getting out of the car.

"Whidbey. Whidbey. Heel!"

Dan Touhcy, a computer geek only a few years older than me, bought this manse from old man Gremlitz a few years ago for $2 million. Now he is here from Seattle full time and I spot him smiling and running around, flapping his arms and calling off his three barking hounds as I wait it out in the jeep, windows rolled up.

These are ferocious animals.

Two are Mastiffs but they look like Pit Bulls to me. Another especially ugly and scarred dog looks like a cross between a Lab and an opossum. All three are jumping up at the jeep. I can't tell if they want to play or if they want to bite me. It seems like both.

Finally Dan gets down to the driveway and he is waving this orange plastic donut thing in the air, trying to get the dog's attention. He catches the eye of the dogs and wings the donut out onto the lawn. All three are off, chasing after the giant plastic donut as if their doggie lives depended on it. I take a deep breath and crack the door of the jeep.

"Hi , Dan."

"I'm sorry, Don," says the gangly businessman, standing somewhat embarrased in his bathing suit and a old tye-dyed t-shirt in his professionally landscaped front yard.

Dan has always seemed like the nicest guy in the world to me and he has never done anything to discredit this theory. He bought his wife this money pit mansion overlooking Jumbala Bay and had it completely renovated. Of course it will always be the old Gremlitz house because the guy who built the place, Gremlitz, threw great parties. And St. Simon is all about cocktail party banter. Dan is low key, but the cocktail talk concerning him is that he must be made of money. That's why I'm here. I want to sell him some tired old $50 and $100 bills that I have buried in peanut butter jars.

I've known him casually for about two years and sort of immediately trusted him. He's got too much real money to fool around with anything too illegal but maybe he'll do me a favor.

He's knows he gets nickled and dimed on St. Simon because he's rich but he's above squabbling about it. He seems sincere and, maybe in a Nutty Professor sort of way, in charge of his destiny.

He is also wondering why I'm standing, uninvited, next to the perfectly manicured red and orange bougainvillea in his driveway on a Sunday afternoon, pretty much drenched in my own sweat.

"Iced tea?," Dan asks, apparently pleased to be interrupted from making deals regarding computers, or something like them, over the telephone.

"Yes," I plead with him. I realize then that Dan probably thinks I want to talk to him about the Jumbala Bay hotel project. From his deck you can see back across the bay and check out the clear-cut jungle spot where the high-end time-share units are proposed. On his wall, in his kitchen, is a picture of how Jumbala Bay looked in 1978, with only a handful of houses that blended into the jungle.

I first met Dan's wife when she arrived at *The Melee* office with five one hundred dollar bills to purchase a newspaper ad. I liked the way she counted them into my hand. The half page advertisment, which we ran for three weeks, asked people to show up to a public hearing on the proposed condominium project. Nearly 100 residents showed up but only about half could cram into the small room where Eustis Smith presides over the Coastal Zone Management meetings. The hotel issue was put last on a long agenda and all of the standing room crowd and most of the seated opposition left before it was discussed.

Dan's wife was pissed. I believe because she had become accustomed to getting what she wants. At the time she was still learning that the people who are "bahn here" on St. Simon, make the decisions, not the people with the money, the way it is done in the United States. It only figures too, because, as Islanders will point out, Dan and his wife, while they don't know it now, won't be here in ten years.

Eustis Smith, however, wants their money to stay and benefit the islanders, so he will listen to them.

While opposed to the project, Dan has been able to keep out of the news stories regarding the proposed hotel. He's smart enough not to step on any toes when he doesn't have to.

"Phoebe is out with her friends," Dan smiles, letting me know his wife will be the family spokesperson if *The Melee* really needs a quote.

"What's up with these dogs, Dan," I have to ask. The coconut retriever has all these open wounds and sores. A chewed up plastic lampshade on the kitchen floor looks like it was supposed to go around his neck. The mutt looked like a vet should put him down but it keeps tussling with the monstrous Whidbey over the toy donut. They look like they could rip right into each other.

"Whidbey is the Alpha Male but this island mutt just won't give in," Dan explains. "He's either stupid or brave, but he won't follow the pecking order."

Whidbey looks twice the mutt's size and is rippling with muscle.

"Good for him," I tell Dan. "he won't take any shit."

"It's just not that easy," Dan explains. "Whidbey knows he is the Alpha Dog and will not back down. He doesn't understand why the mutt won't fall into line. I'm afraid he will kill the mutt. I mean look at him, he has almost been mauled to death, but he keeps coming back for more. I hired a dog psychologist to figure all this out."

I'm dumbfounded. "A dog psychologist?," I ask.

"Why don't you get rid of the mutt?"

Dan explains that he tried.

"We found him nearly dead down on Superman's Beach," Dan said. "Phoebe couldn't bear to leave him at the pound. That was three weeks ago. Now the mutt gets mauled to an inch of his life everyday and I have a dog psychologist on the payroll. "

I was glad Dan saw the humor in the situation. But I was growing rapidly less confident about asking him for one check for a pile of old cash. Still I knew that a Dan check wouldn't bounce and it would be a lot easier to carry down island than a duffel bag full of dirty money.

"I got a situation Dan," I said, as the dogs rumbled by like a three-foot high freight train, literally fighting over the plastic donut. "I got a lot of cash and I need to get out of Dodge quick. Any ideas?"

For some reason it didn't even seem to strike Dan as funny that I would ask him something like this in the middle of an April afternoon in the Caribbean.

"I can't do any money laundering," Dan said without thinking too hard. "The Feds watch me too closely.

He said it in a weird matter of fact way that that I admired.

"I can tell you who probably will, though," Dan said. "Trevor Hartwell has been trolling around for financing for months. He might jump at some of your money for a short term high interest loan."

Dan seemed to forget that I had all but called for Hartwell to be shipped off the island in *The Melee* since he proposed the Jumbala Bay project and that the guy routinely threatened me with lawsuits.

"Dan, I thought you were against that project. You certainly don't want me to get into it do you?"

"Oh, Hartwell will get the financing for it, somewhere, someway" Dan said with the authority of his Stanford MBA. "There are always ways. If you really need to change in that money for a check I know Trevor Hartwell could use some cold cash, I'd rather see you shakedown Trevor Hartwell than anyone else."

Dan amazed me. I liked that he treated me like a player and wondered if he knew about what I had been up to. I shook my head at the craziness of it all as the dogs came whizzing and growling by in a vicious tug-of-war over the donut.

One could see why Dan and Phoebe didn't want to abandon the still unnamed island mutt. Even with one eye appearing to be hanging from the socket, it looked proud and unthreatening at the same time.

"The dog hasn't been brainwashed by all this Alpha Dog nonsense," I said out loud before I remembered how much Dan was probably spending on his pet psychologist. It was a wild dog. It kind of reminded me of Superman. The dog wasn't raised on television movies like Dan and myself. We were raised with a naturally implied pecking order ingrained in our hapless heads.

"How long have they been fighting over that donut?" I asked Dan.

"About three weeks."

"Why don't you take the donut away from them, Dan?

"It wouldn't work, the psychologist says there is always a power struggle. If the donut didn't represent superiority then something else would."

I shook my head and tried unsuccessfully to hold my tongue.

"Dan, just throw the donut away," I told him. "Save that dog's life."

chapter 20

TWO GUYS

Two off- the-rack Caribbean boat guys.

That's what Jenny found. Two guys who had the time and the happy cash to sail to Antigua for Race Week. Guys who made Mt. Gay cocktails so stiff they make you beg for Coca-Cola. These were guys with beer bellies and gold chains that tangled in their graying chest hairs, guys that didn't really care what anyone thought. These guys were good company.

Karl is in real estate. Hell, Karl is real estate on St. Simon. He's sold some houses three times since he showed up from Denmark in the late 1960's. He's still not really rich, but close enough. We are sitting in the cockpit of Sanity his 42 foot Benneteau, anchored in the tucked away Botnay Bay harbor. Around us the hills are dotted with villas and rental homes recently sprouted by the stock market cash from so many snowbirds.

In the cockpit we sit just abaft of a giant stainless steel wheel steering system. I can't help but imagine the aging Realtor bound hands and feet to the racing wheel, spinning around and round and round.

Karl is shady, people will tell you he is a crook. The island has adopted him, however, as a sort of harmless career drunk realtor.

Despite my best instincts I can't help but like Karl. It's like he's kind of a sleaze ball but he is one of our St. Simon sleaze balls, so he is special.

I've seen him out at the bar after selling a house, drank the rounds he bought, and later watched him navigate his inflatable out to his Sanity and nimbly hop on board with a twelve pack in one hand. The next morning he'll be smoking in front of the Post Office, cursing the help and thinking about lunch reservations before I'm even out of bed.

Ron, our other boating partner in this adventure, is curious in a much different way.

He looks like a skinny Telly Savalas and always manages a slow grin, the smile taking so long to actually finish forming that you get bored along the way.

When you talk to him he seems like he is from the American South but I believe he was actually raised in Texas.

As a young man he worked in a slaughterhouse. For years he would go to work and punch cows in the head with a machine that would kill them immediately. It would mess anyone up, but not Ron. Now he is one of the legions of St. Simon dog lovers. His black and white Jack Russell follows him everywhere. Ron's dog is named Annie and is a very cool dog. In fact she kind of runs the show on Botnay Bay Beach, which is home to many island dogs.

A lot of people just know Ron as Annie's Dad. St. Simon is that dog crazy. Both the white and black people here seem obsessed with dogs. There are dog shows, dog walking clubs, pit bulls to poodles this island has them all.

The funny thing about Ron is that he was a cop, for a long time. He fled life at the slaughterhouse to join the Marines. It was a natural step after the military to become a cop. He graduated to border guard and was stationed down in Demming, New Mexico. He saw some shit there he still can't talk about and now he's back with us in St. Simon. The islands are in his soul, he'll explain under the big bimini top on his boat, a classic gaff rigged sloop that rarely leaves the mooring.

Ron likes to invoke Jimmy Buffet and tell the story about how he came down here for a vacation, and was drinking a beer on the beach when he had an epiphany. Ron was 31 then, when he quit the border patrol. He never even went back for his belongings. He had a friend ship him all his stuff. Once he had figured out he didn't want to be a cop anymore he couldn't even go near a uniform, let alone a gun. Now he's 37 and the senior dive instructor for a two-bit SCUBA company. He couldn't be happier.

Ron, along with Jenny and myself, are Karl's crew to sail to Antigua for the annual Race Week regatta. We aren't going to race, just hang out. It should be a good time and a great way for Jenny and me to begin our retirement together.

I tell Karl about the year I went down on a catamaran and the Neville Brothers showed up to play at the after-race party. Karl thinks Jenny and I are just along for the ride and he is glad to have us, especially Jenny who has already let the old man have a have a glimpse of her perky breasts while she scrambled around on the deck of Sanity, preparing the rigging.

Antigua will be a mob scene so we will be able to blend in quickly. If Karl and Ron have enough fun they won't care if we don't come back with them. I'm sure we will be replaced in a matter of hours after we announce our departure from the crew.

We have a duffle back with dirty underwear on top and $18,000 in cash on the bottom. The diamond is in my shaving kit. My savings are still in the ground so I'll be back, someday. A few hundred nautical miles is not far away enough away for me to dig up my stash.

I busy myself readying the boat and am happy to have the busy work to distract my mind. Despite all the craziness, all my mind really wants to do is think about Jenny. In fact it is going to be damn tough not to tell her how deeply I have fallen in love with her. She has quite a knack for savoring a good moment without weighing it down with pollution from the past or hurrying it with thoughts of the future. I don't want to mess with that.

Karl had the boat quite well stocked when we gathered on Monday night. I pulled *The Melee* out of a grocery bag to see my stories about the aliens and Jumbala Bay development buried in the middle of the paper. On the cover Caleb had a story about some tourists finding a bale of cocaine at Sugar Bay. He captured two burly local police struggling to haul the bale away in the bright morning sun quite well. The bold headline which reads **Paradise Lost**? was perfect. The Publisher would do just fine without me.

Our first mate Ron had canceled a full weeks worth of diving appointments and was ready to go sailing. From Karl's Sanity we watched him scramble about on his boat, moored about 200 feet away. He charged the batteries on his sailboat in case the bilge pumps were asked to work overtime. He left his tender tied to his boat and jumped in the ocean. All we could see was a plastic bag and his smile as he sidestroked over to Sanity. He threw me the plastic bag full of t-shirts, Speedos and cash to spend in Antigua.

"Nice story on the aliens," Ron told me, pulling out a satin jacket with a likeness of Michael Jordan which he recovered from the bushes. "Look," he said pulling out a note hand written in Chinese symbols, "I think its a shopping list."

It was a delightful arrival.

Earlier in the day Jenny and I borrowed Karl's inflatable and I lugged our collection of clothes and personal items on to Sanity. It didn't take long to clean out the bungalow. I left most everything for a new tenant I'm sure Judy could find in a matter of hours if she was interested. Whatever Jenny left behind she didn't seem overly troubled by it.

Expectations were high for the trip and the pre-voyage party just sort of naturally erupted, with most of the liveaboards in the harbor motoring over the minute the unmistakable smell of grilling steaks began to waft into the Caribbean night.

Still, I couldn't seem to get one troubling incident from the previous crazy days out of my pulverized brain. I was torturing myself wondering why did the Publisher ask me about picking up a smuggling gig to pay for the villa he hoped to buy with the proceeds he might garner from cocaine I practically gave to him. I told him I found the bales on the beach, just like I did and I don't know if believed me or not. Maybe he was bluffing. I know he didn't know about my route but maybe he had learned something about the cocaine he was going to be selling. Why did he think I knew anything about the line of drug traffic? Maybe I was paranoid again. I was glad to be leaving.

What I knew for sure is that the gentlemen whose reservations I canceled must have wanted to see me about this big dollar issue. They would soon learn about a glut of cocaine on the local market and the Publisher would be linked to me in no time. I closed my eyes and saw the map of the world on my eyelids and felt a pull on my left arm.

"Don't doze off now," Jenny told me. "I've got dinner ready."

On cue Ron stepped up through the companionway doors with a tray of fruity rum drinks.

The steaks were a symphony in the key of delicious and we washed them down with too many Heinekens and too much rum. It was a grand repast and after dinner we sat on the deck like we had accomplished something. I reclined and the stars tried to tell me my future as I gazed up at them from the deck. I was too stuffed to understand their warnings and drifted off into the black to sleep. I slept soundly, dreaming land dreams, and then suddenly awoke, on deck, to a gun shot and the blue bright flash of the morning sun.

Down Island

chapter 21

It was only Karl

The mad Dane was testing his flare gun and the signal was loud and clear. Time to move, parties in Antigua were calling like Budweiser super-model sirens. The previous evening's big meal seemed to have invigorated the mad Dane and I think he already had some rum in his coffee. He might not have even slept.

I tried to focus and saw his grin peek out through his beard. His bald spots caught the sun and shined. He blew on his flare gun like a western gunslinger and lit a cigarette. He vaguely reminded me of a cartoon of Satan.

Looking slightly annoyed by the gunfire Jenny went below to sleep some more. Ron was still snoozing in the v-birth. I raised the mainsail, made sure the inflatable was secured correctly to the stern cleat for sailing. I walked carefully up to the bow to cast off. Karl looked happy that I knew what I was doing, and went below as well.

I heaved the mooring line off, anticipating that the main sheet would fall off to port and walked slowly back along the deck to the big wheel. Slowly the main sheet gathered air. There is a magic feeling to freeing a sailboat without the motor on and I felt it. I spun the wheel and smiled at the mystery.

The wind blows from the east for most of the winter and spring and you can always count on the Tradewinds. I released the selffurling jib before we had gone 50 yards. There was no need to put the motor on and waste fuel we might need in the rare case of doldrums.

I hauled on the sheets, heading to a point just North of St. Thomas. My plan was to run past Roach Harbor and find a nice tack into Sir Francis Drake Channel and past Jost Van Dyke. From there it would be a straight shot around the back side of Tortola into Gorda Sound. We would certainly have another party at the Bitter End in Virgin Gorda as opposed to sailing through the night to St. Martin. From Virgin Gorda we could tack down island to Antigua with a long day and a full overnight sail. It was 9 a.m and I felt like I had the rest of my life before me, the crew remained below deck trying to sleep, my hands tight on the giant wheel.

At noon Karl emerged with a tray of coffee. There was half and half and a shot of rum next to his. Mine was black with a hand held GPS next to it.

"Most of the coordinates are already entered," Karl said, by way of putting me in charge of navigation too. I had already begun approaching Jost Van Dyke and was mentally planning a tack around Beef Island. Time was my friend now. Nobody was waiting for me. Karl put a David Byrne CD on and before long he was telling me a tale a thousand miles long. My thoughts drifted towards days in South America and I wondered if I could get by without having to get all my money from the ground in St. Simon. I was rapidly reinventing myself as the owner of a beach bar on the outskirts of Santiago. Before long I was doing a samba behind the big wheel and Karl was drunk. He was talking madly about the art of the (real estate) sale, women, adrenaline and cheese. I let the words blow astern without grasping their meaning, saturated in my own daydreams.

> *"How does it feel, to be on your own,*
> *When you ain't got nothing,*
> *you got nothing to lose,"*

I fell in love with Jenny all over again when she put on a Bob

Dylan CD down below. The music blared from a speaker on deck and I lost myself in the lyrics. Karl kept talking and while his words were lost on me, his enthusiasm for them cheered me like the promise of a summer day. I skidded his boat well into Gorda Sound before Ron and Jenny made it topside. The crew emerged to witness the depravation that was two ex-pat party boys on this Tuesday afternoon, two veterans of leisure, slugging it out on the front lines.

Ron played the Moody Blues and we all reveled in the way that Karl's fin keeled Beneteau cut through the sea with speed and purpose.

Good boat crew know instinctively to start cooking when Captain and navigator are drunk. Jenny and Ron were no exception, and they began layering a lasagna in Sanity's fancy galley. I kept on peeking in through the companionway doors to see if the pink "banana hammock" Speedo Ron was wearing would register excitement in the close proximity of my young girlfriend. He caught me looking and smiled. I concurred and smiled back.

Jenny played the Stan Getz version of Girl from Ipanema for the third time in a row on the stereo before anyone noticed it repeated. We would make The Bitter End well before sunset, grab a mooring on Karl's credit card, eat, talk, and sleep, quite content that one more precious gem of a day had slipped through our fingers like beach sand while the promise of thousands more remained secure in our cupped palms.

I awoke from another drunken boat party in the pre-dawn hours to realize that what I was sure was boat wakes pitching us back and forth had nothing to do with passing ferries. Jenny managed to remain passed out in my arms despite the pitch from slow rolling waves which were pushed down by a giant storm surge we really should have known about. The swells brought us up and down in the gray dawn and splattered unsecured cookware all over the main cabin. Soon the surfers would be out in force and the North Shore beaches from Hull Bay to Tortola would be dotted with wave riders. The big waves would render tourist spots like Trunk Bay and the

Baths closed for swimmers.

The debate started before the coffee could percolate or the sun could climb the hills of the Fat Virgin.

If we don't leave now, we won't make it to Antigua," Karl reasoned.

A big North swell and a gale from the east will push this boat hard," Ron reasoned.

Jenny and I shrugged our shoulders like a married couple and Karl went to warm up the engine we hadn't touched the day before. It was nice sleeping in Jenny's arms. I think she felt it, she couldn't fake it, I reasoned to myself while I fiddled with the coffee cups.

"I don't know, Don Hunger," Ron said with his slow smile and an eye to the weather.

"C'mon Ron, let's ago sailing," I said since the decision had already been made by Karl. I didn't have the hindsight of the radio warnings like the other mariners who didn't get drunk and listen to samba music the previous day. Had we listened to the forecast we would have never left Botnay Bay, let alone attempt the ambitious 250 mile trip to Antigua.

But the wheel was in motion. It felt very good to bury the rail and feel the spray in my face. Karl gripped the helm while Ron and I double reefed the main. Finally we sailed on just a tiny triangle of jib, watching the squall line race toward us. The combination of turbulent seas, gusty winds and an ominous cloud cover accentuated the deep aquamarine seas. The horizon went on for miles and the wind began to steady. I let more jib out than prudent and we cascaded down waves, nearly burying the nose of Sanity. We hauled the inflatable right up to the stern and miraculously it stuck with us. Ron clocked us at 9.5 knots and my thoughts drifted away from the ties of land toward the magic of nature. Days like this are not for the people that are tied to the land for material reasons of wealth or power but only for those who might breathe in deeply and ensconce themselves in the realm of nature and be fully absorbed by it.

We all seemed to have reached a certain comfort level with the wicked wind when the back stay heaved and snapped. We were literally screaming down a wave when the mast folded forward, the bent steel stick went flying on to the deck with the stays crashing after it. The crinkled mast brought the sails down with it, flinging the broken mast right into the giant maw. Sanity climbed a wave slowly and then crashed her hull down on the metal spar.

"Shiiiiit," screamed Karl charging the forward deck. There was little to save and I gave orders to cut the lines and let the mast go. Karl looked at me, thought about it, and then began releasing the stays.

The gale was manageable by the time we cleared the deck of the busted stays and ripped sails. Karl started the engine back up and we set a course for Fort Bay, hoping to reach the safety of St. Simon.

You gotta love the old diesels, especially the Volvos. They are loud and cranky but once they start they don't like to stop. We all collected some calm as Sanity motored into the swells. The weather to starboard subsided as a wild morning turned into an afternoon of self-rescue.

Karl had come down from such a booze high the implications of losing a mast and head sails didn't seem to phase him. The promise of his bed on St. Simon and an excuse to watch cable and tell adventure stories while the boat was in the yard was plenty for him.

Ron would resume dive instruction, probably by tomorrow afternoon and he seemed to be pleasuring himself with the promise of safety on St. Simon.

I looked at Jenny, and we both shrugged. We still had a shot of escaping together, but it wouldn't be this way.

We made a painfully slow three knots motoring with the weather on our beam and by mid-afternoon we had passed Cooper Island and could see the peaks of St. Simon behind Peter Island.

"We will be at Fatty Kegs by midnight and I will wake up Mark and Gerry personally if I have to so they can make us hamburgers," Karl promised.

His devilish grin turned into a determined pout, Karl never looked more vulnerable with his Foxy's T-shirt all wet and stretched around

129

his beer belly.

Another rainbow unfolded before us, both ends visible in the sea, giving us a view of Tortola and the descending sun. I immediately looked at Jenny. Her head turned to me at the same time and without words we recalled paddling through the colored bars of the rainbow at dawn, how many days earlier had that been?

Jenny looked delicious in the afternoon sun, her brown eyes sparkled and her brown skin glowed. Her lips parted as if she was going to speak.

But it was Ron who yelled from the foredeck, "Get the gaff." His words resonated with panic from the bow, where he had been busy re-securing the boom. His tone made us jump.

"Have you got a fish?" Karl asked.

"Something bigger I think," Ron yelled back.

I grabbed the boat hook and went to the bow. Jenny barely slowed the throttle down as we approached what looked like an upside down yacht tender.

"Cut the throttle," ordered Karl, who had just popped up the front hatch to see the rainbow.

Jenny put the boat engine into neutral and brought a fish gaff to the bow. I watched in disbelief as Ron hauled up what turned out to be yet another bale of cocaine onto the deck. We ripped open the layers of white shrink wrap plastic and Karl and Ron began a nervous but spirited dance of celebration. Again, I looked at Jenny. This was too much.

chapter 22

Plane Plan

Wanna try a plane this time?"

It was about noon. It is impossible really for anyone to sleep till noon in the v-berth of a sailboat while the plastic vessel bakes in the Caribbean sun. But I did it, my body and brain were worn to a frayed knot after our limp back home. Now they both just hurt.

Jenny again was still in my arms, we were sweating so much we couldn't tell who the wetness came from. As soon as my eyes opened we began talking about our next getaway plan.

"A plane might go a little faster," I told her, struggling like an old man to get to my feet to try and get something cold to drink. I failed and fetched us some fetid water..

We had arrived in Fort Bay at about 3 a.m. We motored to an empty mooring with no fuel to spare. Under the stars Jenny and I took Karl's tender over to my O'Day, if only to separate ourselves from the newest bale of cocaine by 25 yards. We passed out in seconds but morning came fast, like we missed the night.

I marveled at the passing of time and fiddled with the always precarious propane stove. The trades were still fresh and the wind blew into the cabin of the Fantasy and blew out the fire. It finally lit and began cooking water for coffee. I saw Jenny's eyes were closed and I thought back to the night before and the deal Jenny brokered for us.

"Buy us out and count us out," that was Jenny's firm message to Karl and Ron, before we got off Sanity.

It is amazing how we had become a team, thick as thieves, as they say, in the course of a week.

Still awake from the night and the taste of the potent narcotic, Karl and Ron were still on Sanity, which remained successfully moored just two boat lengths from our bow. The pair was no doubt rubbing their numb lips and thinking madly about the benefits of the cocaine business.

After we crawled into Fort Bay the previous evening, I told Karl and Ron that they should bury the cocaine, to wait out the glut on the market.

"How do you know there is a glut on the market," Karl asked suspiciously.

I shut up quick.

"I thought you didn't do drugs," Ron said with even more paranoia.

"Hey, be careful how you talk," I told the unlikely drug dealers. "Jenny's a cop."

They looked at me and looked at her. It was late and a lot of strange events had already unraveled in the previous 12 hours. Jenny shook her head, yes, and said that all we wanted was five grand to keep our mouths shut and they could keep the cocaine. I nodded like we had talked about it and Karl went for his checkbook.

The water started to boil and I searched for coffee cups. Jenny opened up her eyes and summed up our situation.

"I guess we are starting to collect some serious cash," she said, still supine in the musty v-berth of Fantasy. I joined her in staring at the shaky handwriting on Karl's check.

I poured coffee and we started counting our fledgling fortune. We had 18 K in a blue duffel bag I used to use for ice hockey gear in college. I confessed to having 30 grand buried in the bush and now we have a five thousand dollar check from Karl. So we were rich, no question about that. And then there was the diamond Judy had given me and whatever Jenny could bring to the table, which I guessed was all invested in her jewelry business. It still hadn't come up in casual conversation.

I showed Jenny the ring for the first time and told her how Judy told us to buy land with it.

"That woman really loves you," Jenny said.

I agreed wondering if she did too.

That is when she asked me to go to New Hampshire with her, to let this dust storm of money and drugs settle for a while. I told her it seemed as good as anywhere else.

"What are we going to do in New Hampshire?" I asked.

"Grow tomatoes," Jenny told me.

After the past few days it didn't sound too far-fetched. I love the good tomatoes, the meaty ones they don't sell in supermarkets anymore.

But at that juncture I was really antsy on the boat and just wanted movement. Grow tomatoes in New Hampshire, sure, just keep the momentum going somehow. I wanted to get off the boat and keep moving.

I guess the big question was who wouldn't be looking for me when we got to land. The police, the Publisher, the drug dealers, probably the Mayor and who knows who else would be stalking the island trying to turn me up.

I started throwing everything in Karl's inflatable, which was still conveniently tied to the stern of the Fantasy. We collected everything we deemed necessary for our first getaway and decided to try again.

I kissed my faithful Fantasy goodbye, smacking my lips on her plastic hull, from my seat in Karl's inflatable. Jenny loaded on as I was pulling at the outboard motor. Ron and Karl screamed and waved at us to pick them up. Fortunately the roar of the outboard motor drowned them out and we buzzed off to shore.

Fatty Kegs was already awash with tourists basking in the crusty ambiance and enjoying the "same day service," the dusty tavern provides. I was bolstered by the site of the French tourist the Publisher and I picked up hitchhiking. She was speeding about the busy bar, delivering beers from a full tray like she had been doing it for years.

We had been too late getting back to Fort Bay to venture into the watering hole the previous evening, but it was just as well. The story of the lost mast had clearly taken a back seat to the found cocaine now and that was the last story that had to get on the Coconut Telegraph.

I saw The Daily News from St. Thomas sitting on the bar. "Cocaine washes up in surf on Tortola, - see page six."

We sat down at the bar next to Elise and her husband, who were clearly having a fight at the bar. She pretended she didn't know me and made small talk with Jenny while I read about the floating bales of cocaine and tried to order food.

"The Mayor's been looking for you," Mark said from behind the bar.

"He came here?," I asked.

"He's been everywhere," Mark said.

This of course was big trouble. Eustis Smith doesn't go looking for white boys in the Continental owned bars. Unless he's really pissed.

"Oh, he left this for you," Mark said handing me an unopened envelope. It just said "Don Hunger" on it.

The typewritten note read as follows:

> *These bales are big trouble.*
> *You don't come and talk to me about this. You go to see Carlos. TODAY.*

The note wasn't signed. I hadn't talked to Carlos in a dozen years. He felt more like a legend than a friend at this point. No one ever talked about his whereabouts. I had wondered if he was dead.

I gathered that Eustis Smith had a role in the smuggling operation. It made sense. He was the most powerful man on the island and he probably received some sort of honorarium or bribe from Carlos.

At any rate it appeared that he was involved. It put the pettiness of our local government skirmishes in a different, irrelevant perspective.

I looked up from the note and saw Elise, clad in yet another absurd print dress, drag her husband away in a huff. Jenny looked at me and said Elise told her that the Mayor had been looking all over for me.

"He's probably looking for you too, now," I warned her.

"I can't believe you slept with her," she told me, smiling coyly.

"She told you that," I countered.

"Her eyes did, so did the look on her husband's face," Jenny said.

Fortunately the subject was dropped when an island policeman entered the bar. The cops never come to Fort Bay so the whole bar turned around.

We got lost in a shuffle of minor and major league local scofflaws, all heading for the back door and vanished easily. I knew my food order would be canceled and it bothered me more than my mounting problems. It wasn't that I was going to starve, but I really wanted a cheeseburger.

"Elise said the Mayor was bothered by something in *The Melee*," Jenny said. I cringed because it couldn't be good. Eustis Smith, aside from this madness about Carlos, might really want to kill me for the trash fire story. Or maybe the Publisher's cocaine story.

Superman could also be pissed about the floating mooring ball story and it would be painful to think I offended the gentle giant. And who knows how the cops felt about the arson of *The Melee* vehicle story. Who knew about any of this.

Time would tell. I just wanted a cheeseburger.

Down Island

chapter 23

Hitching Home

We walked out to the fork in the road with our bags of clothes and money and Jenny put out her finger for a ride to Roach Harbor. The first car stopped for this beautiful girl. She smiled sweetly at the tourist gentleman driving a red rental jeep and climbed into the back seat. The driver was a little disappointed that I would be riding up front with him but masked it well. I glanced back and saw that Jenny had started to cry, steady and silent, before we were even underway.

I kept up appearances in the front seat, answering routine St. Simon tourist questions from the fellow, stuff like, "Do you ever get tired of it being beautiful everyday? What do you do for work? Do you go to the beach every day?"

I struggled through with stock answers and told myself that Jenny couldn't really be a cop, but just a brave, scared young girl.

The driver asked me about the headlines in *The Melee* which he had just seen that morning. He asked me if it was normal for cocaine bales to be washing up by the Sugar Bay Campground.

"It's not too out of the ordinary," I told him.

"What do you do for a living," I asked, hoping to bury the subject.

"Nothing really," he said joking to himself. "I'm a U.S. Customs Inspector in New Hampshire."

I pumped him for information about my new home. It dawned

on me how oblivious I was to having a duffel bag full of drug money between my knees.

Jenny maintained a slow steady sob in the back seat, somehow unable to grasp the absurdity of the situation with the New Hampshire Customs Agent. She resisted the temptation to bite into the small talk about her once homey, home state.

"I hope to grow some tomatoes up in Rollinsford this summer," I told the driver.

SCCREEAACH!!!!!

The driver hit the brakes hard. My face hit the windshield and I felt Jenny's body fly against the back seat. Time froze. A dozen Chinese aliens in the road looked like deer in the headlights.

In shock we looked at each other. About 50 Chinese aliens in all were all over the winding country road, some falling down over the steep hillside and others clamoring uphill into the bush.

It was like running into a herd of goats only they were terrified wordless Chinese refugees.

Amazingly none of them appeared to be hurt. They just stared at the jeep. We could have easily run over a score of them, but the driver braked with amazing strength. None of us could find words as we felt each other for injuries and nodded that we were okay.

The Chinese were in shock too and wondered if they should do something. Some scampered back up into the bush. Some came to see if we were okay. We all looked at each other. The driver was bleeding from the forehead, but looked okay. Jenny and I were fine. I guess I had a little cut on my forehead too.

No cars were coming in either direction. The Chinese were still in wet clothes and were bloodied from the thorns and nettles in the bush. We all got out of the red jeep. Jenny grabbed our bag from between my legs and rifled to the bottom. She started peeling off $50 dollar bills from our stash and giving them to the Chinese. She handed them two bills at a time, careful to get all of them. The Customs Inspector looked at us like we were crazy. He knew he had hit his head and I think he wondered if what he was seeing was really happening.

An open air Taxi Bus came by and Jenny bought the wordless

Chinese a passage to Roach Harbor with three $50 bills.

The transaction happened so fast nobody knew what happened. The Chinese piled into the safari bus and were gone in a matter of maybe three minutes.

Maybe they could get a ferry to St. Thomas and blend in, she reasoned. The suited taxi driver named Blyden was more than happy to go along with the refugee saving effort. The Chinese were sitting ducks for the cops with their wet clothes and confused looks in the open St. Simon country.

I wondered then if I would marry Jenny, and be broke forever. I knew then that if I escaped this madness I would never have to reinvent myself on St. Simon. Maybe I had finally transcended the islands. But first I had to escape, and I had to escape with my future wife.

Down Island

chapter 24

Carlos

Jenny and I had to split up again before we could be together. We had to go to our homest and button things up a little better this time before getting to the airport in St. Thomas.

I had to dig up my money. Now I needed it. But first there were a hundred other details to attend to. I had been on St. Simon for a long time to just leave in such haste.

The first order of business, however, was the slightly shook-up stateside Customs man. We sat him down in my bungalow and Jenny started cleaning him up.

"Why did you give them so much money," he asked Jenny like he had been her friend for years.

"They needed a fresh start," Jenny told him. It would be hard to explain, even to a Customs man, how hard a journey these Chinese refugees were on. How could he understand them fleeing China to be shipped to the Caribbean to eventually wind up enslaved in the Garment District in New York. How could anyone of us really understand their desperation?

I gave him a Heineken and got ready to go.

"My wife's going to kill me," he said, swigging his beer.

I put a shovel in the back of my neighbor's jeep, found the keys in the ashtray and waved goodbye to Jenny and the Customs man

Jenny and I would meet back at the bungalow later, spend a last night on St. Simon and get a 7:15 a.m. ferry for St. Thomas, a taxi to the airport and then maybe a bus to New Hampshire. I could only assume we would be met by someone in a plaid shirt fresh off a milking stool.

Jenny would make reservations. I didn't have a credit card. I did have a passport though, and I hoped it would keep me safe.

I nearly ran over Carlos in the driveway as I sped out. A slender red-skinned man from Bolivia, Carlos hadn't changed in the dozen years since I'd seen him. He got in the car and gave me his hand. We shook softly and he smiled.

"Have you completely lost your shit," Carlos asked me. "Product is washing up on the beaches like driftwood."

"I'm sorry, Carlos."

"I know you are," he said kindly. "It's time for you to go."

"I know."

The money, I learned, for the particular mountain of drugs that just landed on beaches of the Lesser Antilles was all put up by St. Simon real estate developer Trevor Hartwell. He was desperate to triple his investment and start his construction project before he lost everything. When the cocaine went in the water, however, he lost his entire nut.

Carlos let all that slip after I told him I was definitely leaving. I was glad Carlos didn't own the cocaine.

The math must have seemed easy for the developer. Once he got all those drugs stateside their conversion into cash would provide more than enough to begin work on 52 unit, high end, time-share condominium on Superman's Beach. For entirely other reasons, this had been Eustis Smith's pet project for years. Now the financing was gone, which meant the promise of good jobs for natives was gone too.

Hartwell probably would be gone soon as well.

"The Mayor's not mad at you," Carlos said. "He doesn't know you were involved. He's pissed because Hartwell was trying to finance the project with drug sales. He thought it was on the up and up. He wants you to expose Hartwell in *The Melee*. He doesn't trust the Publisher. St Simon is still a small island, the Mayor even knows Caleb is busy trying to sell the washed up cocaine and wants to get the Feds to come and take him away."

"Holy shit," I offered.

"That's how I feel about it," Carlos said. "We have to get off this hot rock, do you have anyplace to go?"

"Yes, I think I do," I told Carlos.

"You may come to Panama with me. We leave by boat tomorrow," Carlos offered. "It's nice on the other side of the Canal."

"I'm set," I said, "but thanks."

"Stay out of touch," Carlos said with a smile, getting out of the jeep.

"Hey, can I take you somewhere?" I asked my old friend.

"Yeah," he said, thinking about it. "Let's go see Superman."

I twisted through the back roads and got out of Roach Harbor and on the road to Jumbala Bay. We drove past the lush hillside where the Jumbala Bay Club would have gone and wheeled down the access road to the beach. Superman had his head in an old Ford pick-up.

"What's the shovel for?" Superman asked us. "Is there some buried treasure I don't know about down here."

We smoked with Superman and laughed about the mooring balls, the floating cocaine bales, Eustis Smith and Trevor Hartwell. Superman was glad to see Carlos.

I felt safe with these outlaws and took them to my hiding place in the woods. I dug at my secret spots while they smoked ganja and laughed. I realized I had a lot of money in the ground. I offered them both plastic Skippy Peanut Butter jars with $10 thousand in old fifties in each. Carlos declined.

"You will need that to take care of Jenny in New Hampshire," Carlos said.

St. Simon is such a small island.

Superman accepted his peanut butter jar full of money gladly. And I was touched that he did.

"I'll only use it for wine, women and song, Donny," he told me.

It was after midnight when I got back to the to the bungalow. Jenny had cried herself to sleep. I re-set the already set alarm clock

143

and crawled in to bed next to her warm body. I briefly wondered again if she was really a cop before I fell fast asleep.

chapter 25

In the swim

It was too early to even speak as we gathered all we could for a life in New England. Nerves rattled us both before the alarm buzzed. I did not register any sleep. I put on my one pair of long pants. Why would I own more. Soon I would need many.

Jenny had only been on St. Simon for two years. She still had a coat. I thought about a snorkel coat I once had. I wondered if it was still in the closet of a friend on Altgeld Street in Chicago. I would certainly need it. I could use it now.

We dressed like zombies and started our trip to New Hampshire without talking. My first sensation walking out the door of the bungalow was one of simple fright. Could I really live in post 9-11 America.

All this washed up cocaine had a strange effect on St. Simon. When we got into town to catch the 7:15 a.m. ferry for the airport, it appeared as if everybody was still up, seemingly from the night before. Eyes glazed over, familiar faces were moving fast, giving the early morning a tense herky-jerky feel, so different from the normal Caribbean pace.

We immediately saw Ron and Karl, of course, drinking coffee in Roach Harbor park. They were sitting with Trevor Hartwell.

"Thanks for stealing our dinghy," Karl yelled by way of good morning.

"Thanks for ruining my life, you will here from my lawyers," Hartwell yelled.

We proceeded on to the ferry dock to get our tickets and there was Eustis Smith, arms akimbo, waiting for us.

"Have you talked with Carlos?"

"Yes, sir."

"Can you do anything about him,?" the Mayor asked, pointing at Hartwell who was still drinking coffee with our boating friends.

"No sir, I'm sorry, sir."

"Your Publisher is going to jail and now you two are under arrest," Smith said.

"No, you're under arrest," Jenny screamed. She seemed hysterical. Now I guess she thought she was a cop, or maybe she was a cop, I was in shock as she began to chew out the Mayor.

All the locals gathered in Roach Harbor began watching this strange scene unfold. The Mayor grabbed me by the hair with his long ebony fingers and tried to wrestle my hand behind my back. Eustis Smith then yelled for the police, like they were supposed to come out from under a trap door in the dock or something. But there were no police, just a lot of tense white people and a few natives trying to get their day going. Everyone looked at the Mayor like he had gone mad.

Then out of nowhere, Superman appeared. He wrapped his giant arms around the Mayor from behind as Jenny bit the hand that clung to my hair.

"Get on dat boat, man," Superman yelled.

We watched Superman continue to struggle with Eustis Smith. Jenny pulled me on the boat, without tickets. We didn't need them, everyone was watching the fight.

Meanwhile, the Publisher, who had been jailed on trumped up charges the evening before was out on bail and was scurrying around the dock in a fury. He was gathering up his latest special issue of *The Melee* which had just been heaved on the dock by the deck hands on the arriving 7 a.m. ferry from Red Hook.

"Save the Bales," read the banner headline on the suspect weekly tabloid.

Caleb started snapping pictures of the Mayor scuffling with Superman. Two native giants, not really mad at each other, but not backing down either. We watched as Superman started to get the upper hand on the Mayor. He pushed the island official back into a group of curious ferry commuters and stoned St. Simonians.

Crowds of people pushed on to the dock to see the scuffle.

Suddenly the Mayor was thrown into the crowd by Superman. The Mayor was pushed right into Karl and two of his female friends and the momentum threatened to push them over the edge of the pier and into the soiled turquoise harbor.

The drop was dramatic, nearly 10 feet. Karl started falling slowly backwards while his arms did airplanes. Then splash. Bodies tangled to see what happened. We had a great view of this circus from the top deck of the Bomba Charger ferry boat. Karl's two busty friends both screamed after absorbing the stumbling Mayor. The pair of screaming women wobbled, then slowly, like Karl, gave in to their imminent plunge over the side of the pier and 10 feet down into the harbor.

This excitement ended the skirmish between the Mayor, who avoided landing in the harbor and Superman, if only because everyone was laughing too hard at Karl and his girlfriends splashing around by the stern of the ferry. Superman and Eustis stopped to look and they started laughing too.

Then we heard the gunshot.

The dozens of onlookers gathered to watch the scuffle between island giants dropped to their stomachs on the pier. Jenny and I ducked on to the metal surface on the top deck of the ferry. On the pier one of the St. Simon policemen fled for safety and many followed. Someone, I thought, really didn't want us to leave. But then we realized it was the big Detroit diesels in the Bomba Charger ferry that were backfiring. Not a gun.

A giant sigh of relief was heaved from the the paranoid crowd gathered on the dock. The range of human emotions we experienced in just those few scant few moments had everyone catching a communal deep breath. We watched Karl clown around in the harbor with his soaked girlfriends. We watched Caleb taking pictures of it all. We saw Superman shake hands with the Mayor, all this as we motored away from the madness that I had long called home.

The airlines wanted $1,000 each for last minute tickets. Neither of us blinked. We just paid the ticket agent with piles of old $50 bills.

The bag full of money got checked with my dirty laundry. I put the giant diamond ring firmly on Jenny's finger. I didn't want the customs agents to think I was smuggling it.

One Customs agent looked at my passport and asked me where I was born. Then he waived us both through with a smile.

Customs turned out to be a breeze. We had crossed the line into a new life. We sat at the gate waiting in disbelief.

A direct flight to Boston, a bad meal and movie.

It was that easy.

chapter 26
Rollinsford, N.H.

The spring flowers fade fast in New Hampshire and the roses bloom and die by mid July. People take life awfully seriously in New England. I knew right away I couldn't fit in and told Jenny as much.

"I gone," I said after a few months in the States.

Life is different in America. Faster in some ways slower in others. It's fun for a while, but not like it looks on television.

Many days I know Jenny remembers the adventures of our last 10 days together on St. Simon and I know she thinks about going back when she isn't cursing my name.

I realize how much I lost but there is an easy sense of victory to sitting on Superman's beach listening to the rag tag band of island musicians celebrate one more day.

That world is gone to Jenny now.

Now she has a farm. It came from the relatives along with a myriad of much more pedestrian tangles and lots of money worries.

Some days, when I worked on her farm, I thought I could do it. I would sleep well and wake to have morning coffee in the garden with Jenny, life seemed like it couldn't have been better.

But she couldn't understand what scared me about it.

All our money was gone fast, of course, invested in the farm. Jenny will sell vegetables and jewelry and barely eke out a living.

She can do a lot of other things too, but I know it will always be a struggle up there. That is just the way it is.

I knew right off I couldn't stay, it just wasn't home, but I tried to roll with it. It was one of the bad days, when the tractor broke and Jenny insisted on getting pregnant, that I decided to get my one-way ticket.

Jenny's landscape now is much different but just as beautiful. Giant stands of white pine give way to the undulating fields filled with corn and tomatoes.

We quickly paid out most of the 50 grand we managed to bring back from the islands. Karl never canceled his check and the airlines never looked inside my peanut butter jars.

The diamond was a fake. Worthless cubic zirconia. We didn't have the heart to tell Judy. She thought it was real and the gift came with too much love to ruin it. The money went fast and I was right behind it.

We talk about it sometimes on the telephone but we can't get it out. I think Jenny wishes she lived the outlaw life a little longer. She doesn't tell me this of course, I just believe she thinks it.

She always asks about the people who have become sort of legendary in her mind. She wonders about all the people, all the drunks, all the hippies, all the smugglers and the low level pirates. I know she wonders if they will show up on her doorstep, all strung out and on the run.

Like I was.

All the charges against the Publisher were dropped after he agreed to sell his newspaper and leave the island.

The paper still comes out every Monday. The Publisher sold it to the same developers he took so much pleasure in deriding. Now the news stories have a decidedly pro-development twist.

Trevor Hartwell was arrested and charged with assault right after the incident at the dock. After he helped Karl and his girlfriends climb up on to the dock he read the headlines in *The Melee* and realized that the Publisher was attempting to link him to the cocaine. He immediately kicked the Publisher in the balls and rolled him into Roach Harbor in yet another outrageous display on the dock that morning. He was taken in immediately but all the charges were dropped against the would be developer when the judge, employing West Indian wisdom, decided that the Publisher deserved a good kick.

While Hartwell is out of the development game, the high-end project is still alive. Hartwell sold the land and permits for the project to Dan and his dog psychologist. Dan's wife Phoebe is busy pre-selling time-shares before they even break ground. They may fit in well on St. Simon after all.

While the beach is still in jeopardy, people aren't immediately worried about the planned development. While financing for the project has been secured, all the political wind behind it seemed to vanish from its sails. After the cocaine controversy, the Governor promoted Eustis Smith to his cabinet and appointed a new Mayor. The new man in charge is a happy fellow named Gene Blyden, the same driver we employed to transport the aliens. Blyden either hasn't been paid enough to support the current Jumbala Bay development plans or else he is against it, because nothing is happening. The rumor is that the development would block his girlfriend's view of the pristine beach. This, most believe, means that the project will be stalled forever.

Or at least until a new administration is elected.

In the meantime Superman, his wife Amy still live on the beach in all of their naked jungle glory.

We all still wonder about the aliens who continue to wash up on the East End. I wonder if the ones we encountered ever found a home. I wonder if I will. Most days I realize I have.

I wonder about Hillary, too, more so when I talk to her.

I know better than to worry about Carlos. He is fine.

I wonder how I could have been so lucky to find Jenny.

She rescued me and I thanked her for it by leaving her safe and bored in New Hampshire.

I still shake my head when I think that she really was working for the FBI when we were lugging bales of cocaine through the bush. I owe her a lot for having the strength to pull me away from all that madness. It's not easy to run. Jenny burned her bridge with federal law enforcement to escape with me. They called it a wash and said they would leave us both alone if we kept out noses clean. When her meager severance package finally arrived she used it to buy a new tractor.

She left law enforcement but I couldn't leave St. Simon. Sometimes I wish I could manage to wrap up the sense of overwhelming calm that travels in the distant swirls of the trade winds and send them off to her.

But I hesitate to contact her from my island in the sun as the more slanted rays of that star begin to signal autumn's arrival in New England. The New Hampshire days become bleak with autumnal death images and I know Jenny finds herself plotting ways to get back to St. Simon. No matter that only five months ago we both thought we might never escape that beguiling rock in the sea.

Now, she finds herself just like so many tourists, wondering how she might get back down island.

chapter 27

Epilogue on the hook

Fred described his love affair in astounding detail, like it had all gone down earlier on this beautiful Caribbean afternoon.

But this particular story he was telling me happened like a dozen years ago, some time after Hugo. I am used to hearing it retold.

Fred and this woman named Crystal were sitting on the beach in Roach Harbor with their backs up against a turned over tender.

Ferry after ferry had left and soon she would have to get on one or be stuck on St. Simon for the night.

They had already talked for hours and there was nothing else left to say. So, nervously, Fred leaned toward her, one hand in the sand for balance.

She closed her eyes in anticipation.

Their lips barely touched at first.

It was perfect. Until the rotted dinghy they were leaning on gave way and they tumbled into it, cutting themselves on the rusty fasteners.

But that was years ago, when like stars crashing through the atmosphere, they shared their first sweet kiss. Fred liked to talk about it.

Today was a fun sailing day and on the way home we began casually lamenting the passing of time. Eventually Fred launched into this rather maudlin tale of his lost love even though he knew my scars for Jenny were far from healed.

"It will always suck," Fred tells me as he fiddles with the mainsail. We are cruising brilliantly, wing on wing, into Fort Bay Harbor on board the Fantasy. I fear Fred has had too much to drink and see him eyeing the Cruzan rum bottle on the galley shelf inside the boat. He always brings up this particular girl when he has had too much to drink.

We sailed the Fantasy right up to her mooring and secured her for the night. I started to think about dinner as Fred continued his lament of lost love. I lit a fire in the steel bucket that holds the big citronella candle and passed it out on the deck to Fred who was too busy with his story to move. I mixed drinks and Fred found an old *Melee* and some leftover floor wax to perk up the blaze. The bug juice in the candle is a great deterrent for mangrove bugs. It is also cheap and dependable light source that doesn't suck the juice from my one 12-volt battery.

In the gloaming some much needed rain arrived out of nowhere. I rigged up the bimini to catch the rain and funnel it into my tanks. Fred grabbed the candle in a can and went below deck with it, the drinks and the tuna sandwiches.

I admit I haven't done much to the interior of the Fantasy, the same boat I held so little regard for only four or five months ago. But since I arrived back on St. Simon I have invested a lot of time, money and energy in the boat. I have added new chain plates and new stainless steel stays as part of a five year plan to make the Fantasy sail again. I want to take it down island to St. Lucia.

The Fantasy is now my home and I intend to make it nice. I commute to work at *The Melee* on a fancy dingy I bought with my share of the stash. I gave Jenny 90 percent of it, well, 80 percent of it, making sure to keep enough for a sweet new dinghy with a dependable outboard motor. I work for developers who bought the newspaper from Caleb. They hate me.

I sold the go-fast speed boat to pay for a long overdue haul out for Fantasy and I bought her some expensive new sails. This boat will never have an engine, not as long as I own her anyway. Too complicated.

Sometimes when you live somewhere as dramatic as St. Simon and consider it home it is hard to verbalize your pride in the place. I'm getting better at it.

In anticipation of more of Fred's stories of unrequited love I made a few more sandwiches by the candle light. You get awfully hungry on the water. Fred played rock and roll tapes and mixed even more drinks. Time drifted by quickly and the dark night became very still.

The battery powered boom box blasted a Little Feat cassette.

"Well they say, Time loves a Hero
But only time will tell
If he's real, he's a legend from heaven
if he ain't, he's a mouthpiece from hell."

Certainly time has passed by all of us here on St. Simon to some extent. While none of us know how much time we have left I believe many of the people on St. Simon are clued into just how precious our time is.

In fact I am somehow convinced that the magical feeling of skidding the water in Fantasy freezes time in a series of magical moments and makes it mine forever.

This day the wind blew us out past Lion Head on the south side of the island as we raced toward St. Croix.

We climbed up the big waves and surfed them down on the quick ride home.

On the ride, with relish, we recalled the old boats.

We recalled the sailing trips too, unforgettable adventures on the high seas. Our life on the water.

Sentiment snowballed, sobriety slipped away and it all sort of wore me out.

Despite the safety of my moored sailboat home I was still not ready to talk about why I wasn't in New Hampshire with Jenny but instead back here on St. Simon. So I let Fred ramble on.

I'm somewhat dumbfounded as he goes on about this ex-girlfriend, Crystal, and their first kiss.

This woman sucked this lovely old hippie dry for years and took off for Hawaii with most of his money. Boy did he love her though.

His eyes danced as he replayed the first time he kissed that crazy woman. The moment was frozen in his mind, nearly tangible. She was stuck there forever, as real as the boat we were sitting on.

The fire crackled and roared in the bucket, a line of soot began rising and started to stain the cabin ceiling. The bubbling wax was starting to overflow from the can onto the teak floor boards.

We both immediately looked at the propane stove and all the other flammable items strewn around the boat. The fire was too big and still growing.

Quick on his feet despite all the liquor, Fred bolted topside, up through the companionway. In one swift fluid motion he snagged the boat hook, jumped back into the salon and speared the fire. Deftly Fred snatched the bucket's handle with the boat hook. Carefully he pulled the burning can up through the companionway doors and with care not to singe the bimini he balanced the flaming can as he walked it out to the open air. Slowly Fred made it to the stern. He looked at me for a nod and then lowered the burning bucket onto the still ocean. The burning can floated upright in the flat harbor.

It was late and the night was still. Venus barely hung in the sky, a new moon had long since set.

The flames were not bothered in the least by the enveloping ocean, but instead seemingly challenged. The can continued to burn brightly against the intense dark of the night sky and the fathomless ocean. There were no waves to tip the burning can, just a slow current to push it off toward the unlit horizon.

In silence we watched the absurdly stable fire in the bucket float away. No electric lights littered the landscape, just the twinkling stars and the burning can on the water. Silently, we watched the drifting light challenge eternity; a lopsided lantern on an impossible journey.

And briefly, time made sense.

Down Island

Down Island